AB TERRA 2021

# AB TERRA 2021

EDITED BY YEN OOI · AND · DAWN OSTLUND

Cover design by Dawn Ostlund.

Published in the United States by Ab Terra Books, an imprint of Brain Mill Press.

Print ISBN 978-1-948559-79-9

EPUB ISBN 978-1-948559-75-1

MOBI ISBN 978-1-948559-73-7

PDF ISBN 978-1-948559-74-4

# CONTENTS

THE LAST FEW YEARS ARE OFTEN DESCRIBED AS DARK TIMES. BUT, WHILE THEIR HORRORS CANNOT BE IGNORED, THEY HAVE ALSO EXPOSED ONGOING suffering and inequality. Likewise, the science fiction community has taken these years as an impetus to turn toward positive visions of the future. Enough of dystopias. Nonetheless, like those age-old inequalities, the call for optimistic imaginaries is not new. As readers and writers of the genre consider what kinds of stories they ought to seek in relation to their era, the question is always: What is the function of science fiction? To invent a radically new future—a release from reality as a kind of protest by escapism, or as a productive tool to think beyond the limits of the past and present? Or to dwell in the muck of history?

I am of the perhaps unpopular opinion that science fiction ought to also set its gaze sideways and backward. To look only toward the future is to turn away from the ways that the past and present shape one's experiences, and even one's ability to imagine what comes next. Moreover, to look toward the future for hope is to assume a linear narrative of progress. Why not treat the past and present as reservoirs of aspiration, in which we might find models, moments, and peoples that inspire? Just as a restrained literary form may generate beautiful invention, one may find creativity as much in the limits of the past and present as in the boundlessness of a radically alternate future.

After all, many of the visionaries in whom science fiction readers seek positive futures went to dark places. Ursula K. Le Guin's short story "The Ones Who Walk Away from Omelas" imagines a city whose idyllic life depends on the torture of a child. The eponymous walkers are those who, unhappy with this state of affairs, leave the city. Le Guin's utopia is far from it—and it also serves, perhaps against Le Guin's instinct, as a metaphor for science fiction's perennial dialectic between past and future, cynicism and hope. Le Guin's heroes leave behind the past and present, the dark truth of the city, in search of a better future, even if it may not exist. But what of the child? Why not stay and fight? Why escape to the boundless world beyond Omelas when, within the dystopian limits of the city, they might actually confront and redress the horrors of their world?

By contrast, Octavia Butler's most optimistic work, her Parable duology, confronts the proverbial child in the city. The duology's future is one of pyromaniacs, enslavement, the carceral state on steroids, and a proto-Trump president. Surely, when Butler had her president declare, "Make America great again," she was not "prescient," as many have recently claimed. Butler was not imagining the future any more than she looked to her past and present. In the series, it is by confronting, and not escaping, the past that Butler's messianic protagonist finds hope. But the past, too, can be a source of optimism. In her Patternist novels, Butler continually revisited cycles of enslavement and colonialism. Yet the series' arguably most hopeful novel is its first entry, *Wild Seed*. Butler's heroine finds peace in precolonial and colonial Africa and, later, early colonial America. Notably, Butler wrote this novel last; perhaps, after all those years imagining a future in tension with the horrors of the past and present, she nonetheless found refuge in history.

My personal route has been to remain in Omelas. As a historian, I study how lawyers and engineers imagined their future; they always drew from their pasts, whether they knew it or not. As a science fiction author, most of my stories occur in the past or present, or in a future still bound by them. In either case, to imagine a radically different future is to erase the present and past of those I study, or of myself—to forget who I am and where I come from.

This is not to say science fiction ought to be only one thing or another. It can be multiple. One can radically imagine beyond the limits of who we are and where we come from. Or one can imagine radically within those boundaries. The genre has always remained open to many forms. The point is to keep open all possibilities.

*Ab Terra 2021* celebrates twelve short stories that explore science fiction in these bounteous permutations. They look forward, radically inventing new futures. But they also look around and back, revisiting motifs of presents and pasts, even if a story takes place years from now. Imagining science fiction that moves beyond conventional narratives requires both tacks. After all, the science fiction of the apocryphal "old white man" sought to produce futures anew out of whole cloth, and it was precisely by ignoring the past that they reproduced its horrors. The stories in this volume are unafraid to revisit history and examine today, as inspiration and warning, as they envision the generations to come.

Haris A. Durrani

AB TERRA 2021

# FOUNTAINS OF PARADOX - BY SD CAMPBELL

All for want of care about a horse-shoe nail.
—Benjamin Franklin, *The Way to Wealth* (1758)

"DOCTOR SRIMAL HEWAVITHARANE?"

The monk regarded the man who held out a hand and had spoken the old name. The man before him was in his forties—the gray hair and wrinkles around the eyes attested to that—but he still held himself with a caged intensity leashed by ramrod-straight posture. He was military, even if his uniform and rank hadn't given it away. This man had the air of someone tenacious and not used to dealing with anything but unvarnished reality.

"I once had that name," the monk said, forgoing the handshake but offering a nod and friendly gesture to join him on a nearby bench.

"I see," Major Alonso Bertram said. He decided not to sit. This wasn't his bag, dealing with monks and such. The view from the monastery was undeniably beautiful—from here, you could almost see all of central Sri Lanka—and in the distance the elevator to the Rail. Nor could Bertram complain about the tropical weather—it reminded him of his boyhood in Sicily. No, it was the preternatural calm of the monastery and monks that sat uneasily on the major's brow. He felt tension here, and he was unsure why.

"So…er…Doctor, what should I call you now?"

"Dharmapala."

"Darma…plapla…"

"Dharmapala."

"Can we stick with doctor, Doctor?"

The monk raised an eyebrow—it wasn't hard to say the name. What game was the major playing? He nodded. "If that makes you most comfortable, Major Bertram."

Bertram's eyes sparkled with amusement. The game was afoot, it seemed. "I don't remember telling you my name."

Dharmapala smiled. "And we both know you can say mine. Shall we call it even?"

"Sounds good, Doctor," Bertram said. "So let me get to it. There's been an incident on the moon. A top secret project you used to lead ran into some…difficulty. I need to mount a rescue, and I need your help."

"Major, I came here to leave behind the chaos of the world," the monk said. "I appreciate your situation, but there must be someone else."

"Nope." The major shook his head, his eyes growing hard. "It's just you. Almost everyone else on the project is dead…due to the incident."

Dharmapala caught himself before the grief and shock overwhelmed him. Gone? Mariko, Jose, Phonse, and that oaf Millardson? Whatever they had done, they didn't deserve this. "What happened?" he asked, trying to keep his voice even.

"Can't tell you here, Doc," Bertram replied, "but we're on a timeline, and I need you to come with me now if we're going to have any hope of saving her."

"Who?" Who had been lucky enough to survive?

"The flight surgeon, Captain Naomi de Beers," Bertram said. "I understand you know her."

The monk stood as well. "Not professionally." He turned to look out at the jungle canopy, an early morning mist rising above the leaves stirred only by the passage of birds. "How long does she have?"

"Seventy-two hours at the most."

"Very well." The monk bowed his head, as if defeated by the universe.

He couldn't leave one of the last people to see his daughter alive to her fate. He had to do something, even if it was just in memory of Samanthi.

○

FOR THE WANT OF A NAIL...

The ride up to the Rail's eastern orbital station was its typical chaos. Dozens moved up and down the space elevator in geosynchronous orbit daily. Of those, there were always some who had never experienced it before, and many seemed to revert to their inner ten-year-old selves.

Major Bertram tried not to be annoyed by them. He tried not to be annoyed by how slow the elevator ride seemed to be. He tried not to be annoyed by the monk's stubborn silence.

"Dharmapala. What does it mean?" he asked.

"I see. You can pronounce it."

"Well then, Dharmapala, what does your name mean?"

"It means 'Protector of the Dharma.'" The monk continued looking out the window of the elevator car. From here, he could see the whole of Sri Lanka—small enough to cup in two hands. "An ancient ancestor of mine picked that name when he committed to follow The Path. I chose it as my Dharma name when I committed to change my path."

"And now?" Major Bertram asked. "Now that you're coming back into the world?"

"Call me Doctor, if you like," Srimal said. "Or Srimal. Or Doctor Hewavitharane."

Bertram held out his hand again. "Alonso."

Srimal shook it.

"Look, Doc, I'm sorry to have had to do this to you. Trust me, if there was anyone else I thought I could shanghai for this, I would."

Srimal nodded. "I know," he said quietly. "We never know what roads we are fated to walk, and what even the smallest of things can do to make us walk them."

"For the want of a nail…"

Srimal raised his eyebrow. "Pardon?"

Bertram sighed. "I can't tell you everything. No details until we get to Copernicus Base, but according to Doctor de Beers, it was an oversight in the calculations or specifications or something. That's what she said: 'For the want of a nail.'"

"You're in contact with her?"

"Not currently—and with the OC3 line to the labs down, we were only able to receive her message, not transmit back to her."

Srimal could see the major clench his fist in frustration. This South African man of action was currently powerless. It clearly rankled.

"What did she say?" Srimal asked.

"All I can tell you at the moment is that she only had forty hours of air twenty-six hours ago." Bertram's fingers were clenching and unclenching subconsciously. "She put herself into a hibernation coma, but she'll be out of that in the next twenty-four hours, approximately."

"If we don't get to her before she wakes up and exhausts the rest of her air supply…"

They both knew what that would mean. The tragedy, of course, would be compounded for those who had authorized the project, as they would have no survivor to question or blame.

The men lapsed into silence for a time.

"I met her briefly after the Armstrong Dome disaster. How did you meet her?" Bertram asked as they approached the top of the elevator.

"Doctor de Beers?" Srimal asked.

The major nodded.

"She was…a close friend of my daughter's. How we met is a long story."

The elevator car slowed to a stop.

"Top floor," Bertram quipped. "Everybody out."

Srimal followed the major's purposeful strides. From here, they would need to take a hopper down to Copernicus. It would give Srimal a chance to bathe, rest, and change from his robes into something more practical.

Srimal's thoughts though were miles and years away.

o

"YOU READ CLARKE?"

Srimal looked up from his novel and smiled to the young lady who served him his drink. In his hand was *The Fountains of Paradise* by A. C. Clarke.

"He's a favorite where I come from," Srimal said as he paid her for his soda. "So, of course, I've never finished a single book of his."

The honey blonde laughed. "Well, I hope you enjoy this one," she said as she left.

Srimal had to admit, he did enjoy watching her go.

It was summer break, and he'd decided to take time away from his thesis at MIT to get to know the world a little bit better. He'd done that every year since he started university. This year it was Canada—Calgary specifically. The weather was hot, which he was used to, and dry, which he was not. He had decided to stick to soda as a way to rehydrate, as it was cheaper than water and caused fewer complications than alcohol.

On that scorching July day, Srimal was perched on a stool on the patio of one of the establishments that lined the Stephen Avenue Mall, a pedestrian mall in downtown Calgary. The holiday for the country's founding was over, so most of the Canadian flags that had decorated the mall had been taken inside and replaced by bales of straw and plywood cows and horses.

*There is kitsch,* Srimal thought, *and then there is this.*

He turned back to his book. Despite his lifelong desire to work in space as an engineer, Srimal had never taken to science fiction, at least not the so-called classics. He found Asimov and Heinlein too childish and Clarke too dry. But one couldn't claim to be a "nerd from Sri Lanka," as his research partner liked to put it, without at least trying to read Clarke.

Srimal had picked *The Fountains of Paradise* because of its deep ties to Sri Lankan legend and history. He was still having a hard time getting through it.

Cowgirls in tight denim short-shorts weren't helping.

Srimal shrugged, dog-eared his page, and finished his drink. Maybe he could find someplace less distracting, farther down the mall. He turned without looking and bumped into a pair of young women who had been eyeing his table and rushed forward to claim it.

"Oh, excuse me!" he said, bending to pick up his book and a cell phone that had dropped near one of the women. He blushed and handed it back to her as her friend, now sitting in the seat Srimal had vacated, laughed behind her hand.

"That's quite all right," the woman he'd run into said shyly. "I'm sure it was my fault."

"Not bloody likely," her companion said with a noticeable upper-class British accent. "Come on, Ginny, we've been waiting for hours."

Shrugging again, Srimal stepped off the patio and onto the mall, but before he got far, he turned around and observed the two women in conversation. He recognized the body language, and, while he couldn't hear much over the pedestrian noise, what he did hear was strikingly familiar.

"Excuse me," he said, having walked back to the patio boldly and leaned on the metal rail beside their table. "You two don't happen to be from Sri Lanka?"

The taller of the women, the one he hadn't bumped into, raised an eyebrow. He extended his hand. "I'm Srimal Hewavitharane."

She returned the gesture. "Anupama Abeyesundere."

That was how Srimal remembered meeting his wife.

o

COPERNICUS BASE HADN'T CHANGED MUCH SINCE he'd last been there a decade before. Srimal and Major Bertram arrived by hopper midway through the base's day cycle, and on arrival Srimal was given a key-card tablet that would allow him access to certain compartments and also act as a calendar and communication device.

"Uh, sir," the base security staffer said as Srimal turned away, "you need to deposit your cellular devices with me here."

"I don't have any," Srimal said evenly.

The young man looked at Srimal and then at the major. Bertram nodded, and the staffer shrugged, allowing the two men to pass into the main section of the base.

"So, are all you monks anti-tech?" Bertram asked as they walked toward the visitor's quarters.

"No," Srimal said with a slight smile. "I just always wanted an excuse to get rid of them. Connection to the world a thumbprint away was too connected to material things for me personally."

"Huh," Bertram grunted. "Well, Doc, I have to catch up with my boys now that I'm back lunarside. The briefing is in two hours. I assume you'll be able to find your way?"

Srimal smiled. "Yes, Major. Finding one's way around the base is just like remembering how to fall off a bike."

The major paused, looked at Srimal, and then barked out a laugh. Shaking his head and still chuckling, the soldier headed off, leaving Srimal to find his assigned quarters.

They were smaller than he remembered, although, thinking back, maybe the quarters for married staff had been larger. Certainly, his quarters at Project Paradox had been much larger. Then again, his quarters in the monastery were very much smaller.

He had showered and slept on the hopper, and so he stepped out from his quarters to find the cafeteria and a bite to eat before the briefing. When he and

Anupama had been stationed here, it was busy, but he didn't remember Copernicus ever being this crowded.

Having selected a salad and fruit juice from the offerings in the cafeteria, he took his tray over to a stool that looked through the quadplex quartz viewport. Earth hung, a waning gibbous planet above the gray lunar regolith. He thought back through the many years since he'd last done a moon walk and found himself rather anxious, even claustrophobic.

So much had stayed the same, but so much more had changed.

He was no longer the brilliant and eager engineer, or even the strong and steady leader. Looking out across the moon's desolate landscape, which seemed to cup that beautiful blue home of his, made him feel small and empty inside.

Had he left for the monastery to escape this hollowness? Or had he escaped from the monastery to be left with it?

Over a decade after he'd tried to let go of his attachments and just be, he wondered how much of himself there was left. If you took away all that Srimal Hewavitharane had lost and even the emptiness of the loss itself, was there anything left?

*For the want of a nail…*

*…Srimal was lost.*

DESPITE THEIR FAMILIES FINDING IT SCANDALOUS, Srimal and Anupama didn't get married until after they had both finished their doctorates. Srimal had finished his degree first and then moved to Calgary for the final couple of years of Anupama's. They returned to Sri Lanka several times over those two years, always to meet more family who hadn't yet been introduced to the new fiancé of however-something-removed-cousin-whichever.

Srimal didn't mind it, but he had soon discovered after meeting Anupama that she was far too free a spirit to be willing to play that game for long. So most often he and his family became the excuse for why she couldn't come visit old-auntie-whoever. In those days, it had been fun and charming.

After they completed their graduate work and had a proper Buddhist wedding, the couple then had to figure out what opportunities they would pursue. Srimal had pushed for Anupama to chase her career. He insisted that in this day and age of instant global communication, he could work from home, or from anywhere. She found it difficult to determine what she really wanted to do, however. A degree in advanced mathematics didn't leave one with a whole lot of options beyond teaching.

Luckily, a former professor of hers, a theorist at the Perimeter Institute in Waterloo, had started work on a crazy theory of space-time manipulation. The opportunity to open new doors in space and time—at least theoretically—tempted the couple back to the colder climes of Canada.

For Srimal, it was an exciting time. He'd been able to land a job teaching at the University of Waterloo, and, in hopes of eventually receiving tenure, he began working on some advanced magnetic confinement designs he had tinkered with while at MIT. The hours were long, the teaching was dull and the research mostly underfunded, but he felt like he had some skin in the game, while his brilliant wife and her mentor shook the academic world with their crazy theories.

What they had intended as a five-year sojourn in Canada before returning home to start a family ended with both of them being offered positions on an advanced research project at Copernicus Base on the moon. For years, Anupama would tease Srimal by saying to friends, "He was only on the moon because of me. We could have had any of a dozen engineers with the same qualifications. It was his shoe size that sealed the deal for me."

Sometimes it was the size of his ears rather than his shoes, but Srimal was never embarrassed. Indeed, he loved the devilish gleam she got in her eyes when she told that story and looked at him. It was the same look she gave him a year later when he found her sitting on the bed in their quarters, wearing a satin robe and holding a small penlike object.

"Guess what I missed," she said.

"You're…" he trailed off as he saw the gleam in her eyes.

"Yes, my love," she said as she stood and let the robe slowly fall to the deck. "Now come and ravish me before my belly gets too big for anything kinky."

That was how Srimal remembered being told he would be a father.

○

"I want to start this briefing by giving a warm welcome to Doctor Hewavitharane, who has joined us on short notice from Earth," the director said once they were all gathered in the briefing room. "Doctor Hewavitharane was the chief engineer of Project Paradox up until five years ago." He nodded at Srimal. "We are very grateful for his offer to lead the rescue team."

The director touched a button, and a screen flickered to life, showing a 3D representation of the Project Paradox facility and its critical gateway, commonly referred to as Paradox, or the Paradox Gate. Many of the compartments were colored red, and a single one was colored yellow.

"This is what we know," the director said. "Thirty-four hours ago, the initial Paradox opening was attempted, but we immediately lost contact with the facility. Without hard lines into the systems, we don't know the status of the gate, although according to the sole survivor it seems stable."

He touched another control, and a young blond woman's photo appeared. "We have a single survivor—Captain Naomi de Beers, the project's flight surgeon. She was able to contact us though an emergency transmitter and indicated that she believes the accident was caused by an electrical arc passing back in time through Paradox, triggering the accident and making the Paradox Gate self-sustaining." The director waved down the murmuring voices. "She has suffered a head injury, so we cannot accept or dismiss her report at this time. She's put herself into a temporary hibernation coma so she can subsist on the remaining oxygen, which would otherwise run out before we can reach her."

"Doctor Hewavitharane." The director nodded at Srimal again. "You're the only person here with intimate knowledge of the construction of the facility, its equipment, and the Paradox Gate itself. This is why we need you to lead the rescue team. You know the space better than we do, and you should be able to find an open route to Doctor de Beers."

"Yes," Srimal said, standing up. "I have several ideas that I can lay out, but first I want to clarify something."

The director sat down, and the room fell silent.

"Paradox wasn't designed to be a time machine," Srimal said. "No matter what Doctor de Beers believes. It is a highly dangerous event horizon, and if you approach it—especially if it is now self-sustaining—you run the risk of absorbing a large amount of energy very rapidly." He paused and looked around for effect before he added, "Which would kill you." Srimal continued, "Doctor de Beers seems to be a meter and a half in front of the portal framework, within an area known as the Pit, so the medical staff will need to stabilize her and move her quickly. No one should approach the equipment any closer than that."

"And what about shutting it down?" a voice called out from the back of the room.

Srimal sighed. He had known deep down that this could happen. Anupama, however, had been very insistent: it was not possible for an energy arc to propagate backward and initiate a self-sustaining reaction. This disagreement had been the greatest cause of stress in their marriage until Samanthi…

"If it's self-sustaining," Srimal said, "we may have no way of shutting it down. If—and it's a big if—it is powering itself from the future, I have no idea how we would stop that."

Major Bertram stood up. "We'll cross that bridge when we get there. Now, Doctor Hewavitharane, let's see your entry route suggestions."

o

BY THE SECOND TRIMESTER, THEY HAD DECIDED TO return to Earth. It wasn't that giving birth on the moon would be unsafe—several very healthy babies had been born off Earth's surface in the last decade—but Anupama had suddenly felt the need to have family around. In those days, it had been amusing and charming.

Being away from Copernicus didn't stop their work, however, and each corresponded with their teams on a regular basis. The theoretical team that Anupama was on had been able to expand on the underlying theories to an extent that they were now guiding the development of the control software for the portal.

Srimal was one of the senior leads of the engineering team, and they had just completed design work on a pico-portal that would allow them to test the theory on something the size of a molecule.

"It would scale, of course," Srimal told one of Anupama's cousins the night Samanthi came into the world. They were renting a small apartment in Colombo, and the last month had been a constant stream of aunties coming to see to the health of their niece. It was up to Srimal to entertain their husbands.

"Srimal's a terrible entertainer," Anupama had said at the start of one night's gathering. "He's an engineer."

"I understand that's how they started with the cable design for the elevator," a cousin had said to Srimal several hours later. "A single long crystal grown in orbit to test the idea."

"Exactly," Srimal replied. "What we're talking about with this portal is the ability to transmit quantum data instantly across space-time without needing entanglement or any other spooky action at a distance."

"What would happen if you started sending a stream of particles?" the cousin, himself an engineer, asked. "Wouldn't you have a…particle fountain on the other end?"

"Not necessarily. Anupama's most recent work shows that different angles of entry—different vectors—would arrive at different times or places, depending on the velocity of the particle at the time it entered the portal—"

The phone rang. "Oh, excuse me," Srimal said, standing to go to answer it.

"Srimal!" Anupama called from the other room.

"I'll pick it up!" Srimal shouted back.

The phone continued to ring.

"Srimal!" Anupama shouted.

"I've got it!" Srimal said loudly. "Hewavitharane residence."

"Srimal!" Anupama screamed.

Then came the cry of a child taking its first breath.

That was how Srimal remembered his daughter being born.

o

"I STILL DON'T UNDERSTAND WHAT THIS THING IS," Major Bertram said as the rescue team took a mandatory rest break, crouched in the partially collapsed tunnel of the Project Paradox Facility's East Wing.

"They made it all top secret after I…left. So I don't know what you know or were told."

"Precious little," the major said. "I no longer think it's a communications array, though."

"Actually, it is, or was intended to be," Srimal said, sipping some tepid water from his suit's drinking tube. "When we discovered we could scale it to man-sized objects, there were suddenly a lot more possibilities."

"Like what?"

Srimal picked up a shattered piece of foam ceiling tile and poked a hole in it with his finger. "Well, Major, say this tile is our regular space-time, and I've just opened a hole in it using a lot of energy."

"Got that so far," came the sarcastic reply.

Srimal ignored him. "If you look straight through, you see whatever is on the other side. If you shoot a laser through, it will shine directly ahead. Now, angle the laser slightly, and it goes to shine at a different angle. Now imagine I could speed up the photons in the laser…"

"Nothing goes faster than light," Bertram snorted.

"For argument's sake," Srimal said. "If I make the photon go faster, it goes farther after entering the hole. Now imagine there is gravity on the other side of the tile, dragging the photon back to the tile. If you go slow enough, the photon ends up falling backward."

"You lost me."

"What if you enter the hole at a shallow angle and go so slowly that you loop back on yourself?"

"The photon goes back in time?"

Srimal nodded. "That is a distinct possibility, at least theoretically."

Suddenly the ground under them rumbled.

"What the—" Bertram shouted as debris pelted him.

The entire floor jumped, and Bertram was smashed to the ground by a chunk of concrete and rebar. The pinned major shouted in anger.

"The reactor's magnetic fields must be collapsing. When the containment fails, it'll flatten what's left—including the Paradox Gate." Srimal pointed to the two medics on the team. "Follow me as soon as you have the major free and stabilized," he commanded as he latched one end of his tether to a hallway stanchion. "I'll find Naomi, and then we'll get out of here before it turns molten."

The medics nodded as Srimal disappeared into the dusty darkness.

o

"YOU KNOW WHAT THAT LOOKS LIKE?" ANUPAMA asked Srimal, looking at his most recent designs. He shrugged, so she continued, "Like a fountain. The way the polarizing conduits arc up and across the deflection plates for the portal."

Srimal laughed. "A fountain of what? Paradox?"

"Of course," his wife said, her arms around him. "Like that stupid book you never finished."

"*The Fountains of Paradise*?" he asked.

"Yeah. It keeps appearing on our bedside table," she said, playfully nibbling his ear.

"I love that book!"

The couple turned toward the voice to see their daughter Samanthi and her girlfriend Naomi mimicking their pose. Anupama scowled, but Srimal laughed.

"If you like that book so much, Samanthi, why do you keep putting it back on my nightstand?"

"Well, it's your book, right?" She suddenly cringed. "Hey, that tickles!" she said, pushing Naomi's face away from where she had been licking Samanthi's earlobe.

Srimal laughed, a deep booming sound that seemed to rattle the windows of the small apartment. Samanthi smiled as Naomi giggled, but both grew more serious at Anupama's severe look.

"You two know that some people would do terrible things to you if they knew who or what you are," she said.

Srimal put a hand on her shoulder, willing her to calm down.

"Lesbians, Mom," Samanthi said, with her own scowl now. "It's not a dirty word."

"No one is saying it is," Srimal said, "but your mother is right—overt displays of affection might not be a good idea, considering the political situation."

"Yeah, well, screw them," Naomi shot back. "Bloody conservative trash."

"Anyway," Samanthi said, changing the subject, "we're going to grab the train back to Trinco. Naomi's brother is staying with us for a couple of weeks, and we should be there when he arrives."

"You should just stay the night with us," Srimal said. "Take the train in the morning."

"I'm not a child, Dad." Samanthi was annoyed. "I don't need a sleepover."

"Be careful," Anupama said. "Please, just be safe."

"We will, Mom," Samanthi said, hugging her parents goodbye. "We'll be very good and very safe lesbians."

"We even have a safe word," Naomi stage whispered. Srimal shook his head and shooed them off.

After they left, Anupama sat on the couch, brooding. Srimal sat beside his wife and took her hands in his.

"I don't have anything against them being…lesbian," she said quietly. "I'm not…It's not an issue for me. I just worry that…"

Srimal nodded. "Samanthi knows that. She knows you love her and accept her and you're only trying to express wanting what's best for her." He shrugged before adding, "But she's also a college girl, and if she's anything like her mother, she would have no problem letting a strange man from Sri Lanka take her on the Tilt-a-Whirl at the Calgary Stampede."

"Well, not any man," Anupama said with a small smile as she rested her head against his chest. "She's our only child, Srimal. I don't know what I would do if anything happened to her."

"Nothing will," he said. "I promise. Let's go to bed."

It was a promise he would forever regret making, because it was one he couldn't keep. He had known it the moment the phone rang at four the next morning. By the time they reached the hospital, Anupama had stopped crying. Now she just seemed numb.

When they were escorted in, Naomi broke away from the police officer she had been speaking with and ran over to fling her arms around Srimal. "Oh God, Srimal, we should have listened. We should have stayed the night. If I could do anything different..."

Her blond hair was matted with blood, and her whole body shook with her sobs. Srimal held her at arm's length for a moment, and she looked up into his eyes, her grief mirrored in his own.

"I'm okay," Naomi whispered, hoarse. "It's *her* blood."

Another flood of tears came, and Srimal found himself rooted, unable to move lest he disturb this shaking leaf that clung to him.

"I said…I said that…that I could…you know…identify her…so you wouldn't…"

"Thank you," Srimal said. "But we need to see her, too."

He felt Naomi nod, and he looked up, suddenly unable to meet his wife's eyes. An orderly and a police officer escorted them to the morgue, where he found Anupama waiting. He reached out to her, but she just looked at him, and in her eyes he didn't see pain or grief, just hatred. From that moment onward, she never touched him again.

Srimal looked down at his daughter's body. She looked so small and pale. So different from the young woman who had been full of verve and life only a few hours before. The impostor before him—it couldn't have been Samanthi, her skull crushed and her hair pulling away from her scalp. She had a birthmark, a small heart shape just to the left of her navel. He had to check…

He reached for the bloody white sheet that covered her, but the orderly stayed his hand.

"You don't want to, sir," she said. "They cut her pretty badly after they…had their way with her."

Suddenly, something in Srimal snapped. He screamed his rage at the universe and slammed his fist into the cooler door. The hospital would tell him later he'd broken three knuckles, but he never remembered any of it.

That was how Srimal remembered his daughter's death.

o

A BLINDING LIGHT PLAYED ACROSS HER EYES, AND she coughed as a cloud of dust suddenly seemed to envelop her. How long had it been? Had she been able to stop it? Was everyone safe?

No. No. No.

"Naomi," a voice behind her called out. "Are you there? It's Doctor Srimal Hewavitharane."

Naomi twisted to look at him and cried out. Something jagged was sticking out of her side, and the pain overwhelmed her. When she regained focus, it was to see an old friendly face.

"God, Srimal, how are you here?" she asked. "I thought after…You were in Sri Lanka." She paused. "Am I dead?"

He shook his head and muttered some words into his headset. "You're as alive as I am," he replied gently, removing rubble from her legs.

"I heard about Anupama. I'm sorry."

"I know, but it was her choice. I made mine. Hers included a bottle and not me. I'm sad for her, but perhaps she found peace in her own way."

"Srimal," Naomi whispered, coughing as movement stirred up the dust. "It works."

He paused. "What do you mean?"

"The time hypothesis you and Anupama always talked about—it worked."

"How do you know?"

"I came back. Things were different this time."

The medics crawled in through the passage and began to assess Naomi for transport. Srimal stood and looked into the Paradox Gate. It was featureless, but suddenly Srimal began to see opportunities within its obsidian depths.

"If I could do anything different..." Srimal heard a much younger Naomi de Beers say in his memory.

Could they do something different?

Could it be different this time?

He stepped closer to Paradox.

"Srimal, don't..." Naomi reached out to him, but he was enraptured, looking at the ebony portal. He glanced back at her as the medic closed his kit.

"She's okay to move, sir."

Srimal nodded. "Then get her and Major Bertram back to base and evacuate the rest of the facility."

"What are you going to do?" the medic asked.

"I'm going to see if I can shut this down," Srimal lied.

"Srimal, you don't know if it will change anything!" Naomi cried out. "I loved her—you know how much I loved her, but you can't do this just for her!"

Srimal looked at Naomi and smiled calmly. "You said, 'Things were different this time.'" He pulled his key-card tablet from his pocket and began calculating entry vectors. "Maybe I can make things different this time, too."

"I only meant by minutes, Srimal. You're talking years…years ago back on Earth!" Tears were streaming down her face. "Please, come with us. Don't let this false hope destroy you, too."

He nodded to the medic and stretcher bearer, and they picked up Naomi and carried her from the complex. He could hear the echoes of her pleas fading as if in a dream, or a meditation.

Yes. Perhaps that's what this was. He was finally free from his worldly attachments. There, on the other side of Paradox Gate, were Samanthi and Anupama and a life that had been stolen from him. And if this didn't work, what would it matter? For the opportunity to see her alive again—see them both alive again—he would brave this Fountain of Paradox, gladly.

He watched the timer tick down.

He closed his eyes.

He leapt.

*For the want of a nail…Srimal was found.*

# THE SOMERSET PROVISION - BY THOMAS PACE

IT WAS WELL PAST MIDNIGHT BY THE TIME ANDERS FINALLY MANAGED TO GET OUT OF THE OFFICE. IN THE ELEVATOR, HE PULLED HIS BUZZING PHONE FROM his pocket and switched it to do not disturb.

When he got to Sloan's, he steadied himself down the steep cast-iron stairs still wet from the rain. As he stepped through the door and into the pub, he felt the phone buzz in his pocket. Puzzled, he retrieved it and saw the red lettering across the screen announcing the call, EMERGENCY—MICHA. Anders declined the call and stuffed the phone back into his pocket.

He saw that Stone, Pierce, and Ahmani were already sitting at their usual corner of the bar. As he approached them, he felt the knot in his chest loosen, and for the first time in almost twenty-four hours, he took a full breath.

"Get this man a drink!" Stone shouted to the bartender as he slid over one stool to make room for Anders.

Anders received his Scotch and quickly tossed it down. As the bartender refilled his glass, the quartet sank into stunned silence.

"So," said Pierce, breaking the dismal spell, "how was your day?"

They laughed a much-needed hardy and heavy laugh, embellished with a sense of release. You could always count on Pierce for comic relief.

"Anything new?" Ahmani asked, her speech slightly slurred with drink.

Anders shook his head. "Nothing."

"Got to be terrorism, right?" said Stone in a tone that sounded more like a wish. "Mass self-destruction?"

Pierce called from behind his hands as he worked to rub the disbelief from his glassy eyes. "What the hell? Will somebody please tell me what the bloody hell?"

"I just don't understand how it's possible," said Stone.

"Goddamn Somerset Provision," Anders said.

"Every single unit?" Pierce shouted.

Anders was pretty sure that there was a tear in the corner of Stone's eye. And why shouldn't there be? Stone had been working at Morrow since it was little more than a handful of grad students in Colten

Carr's Palo Alto garage, cobbling together a quaint prototype of what would eventually be the most celebrated piece of commercial technology since the introduction of the television or the iPhone.

If you had asked any of the young men and women back then, thirteen years ago, what they were doing in that garage, they would have undoubtedly told you they were building a robot. And while that was technically true, tonight, from the stool at that bar, the notion seemed quaint.

Of course, the Domo was a robot. It was not the only, nor even the first, artificial bipedal humanoid on the market. The CY-5 was in many ways very similar in design. Aluminum carbon hybrid endo-frame skeleton powered by hydro-fission. The newest versions even had the fiberualic musculature system similar to that developed by Stone and Pierce in the Kinesiology Department at Morrow for the Domo almost a decade earlier. These synthetic muscles contracted and elongated like biological muscles and were still considered one of the more celebrated advances in robotic realism. Despite the similarities, however, the two robots were remarkably different.

The phone in Anders's pocket buzzed again. He found it ironic that Micha had called him more today than she had in all the time since their divorce. He pulled the phone from his pocket only long enough to silence it. When he looked up, he saw the others were leaning over the bar staring at him attentively. "Sorry," he said. "My ex."

The little air that was left in them deflated. They passed around that look of disappointment once again.

Ahmani's phone, faceup on the bar, buzzed to life. She scooped it up and answered. A dire look spread across her face. "You're kidding…Anything else? Okay, keep me posted." She set the phone back down on the bar and took a deep breath. "You guys are not going to believe this," she said as she peered over her glasses. "The media is referring to it as a mass suicide."

"Suicide? Oh, this is bad," said Pierce, looking over to Stone. "They're going to be calling for our heads."

"They'll go after Carr," said Ahmani.

"You think that will be enough?" Anders asked. "They might start with Carr, but they'll eventually work their way down to each of us."

"The truth of the matter is," Stone said, "all this upheaval? It's actually the product of a job well done."

"Oh, for Christ's sake," Ahmani scoffed. "What does that even mean?"

"Think about it. All this panic and outrage is really a reflection of the emotional investment people have in these things."

"That's the worst silver lining in history," said Ahmani.

"Don't get me wrong," he continued. "It's a terrible thing for everybody. I'm not saying it's not. But isn't it also an illustration of how much our creations are loved?"

"Were," she said. "Were loved."

"He's right," Pierce said. "I don't think any of us could have imagined that people could possibly become so attached to a machine."

"I don't know. People have always been attached to their machines, especially Americans. Their cars, their TVs, their phones."

"Exactly," countered Stone, agreeing with Ahmani. "But not like this. Even in a culture well versed in emotional dependency on devices and machines, the Domo stands above."

Stone was right. The public reaction to Morrow's 'thinking robot' fit safely into the category of a cultural phenomenon. Those who bought the first line were quickly enamored, reporting that the Domo not only seemed to hear but actually listened.

Ahmani's phone buzzed again. She snatched it, and the three men stared at her as she gazed at the screen and scrolled. "Oh, for Christ's sake," she said half to herself as she rolled her eyes.

"What is it?" asked Stone.

"Nothing, really. They managed to officially confirm the activation of the Somerset Provision."

"Well, no shit," said Pierce.

"And that's it?" Anders asked. "No explanation as to why?"

"I guess Anders owes Senator Somerset a long-awaited 'I told you so,'" Stone said.

"Oh my God, the irony," said Ahmani.

Anders ignored the buzz in his pocket.

"You very well might get your shot, Anders," Stone said. "Although this time it'll probably be in front of a grand jury instead of a committee hearing."

Senator Gordon Somerset was the head of the U.S. Senate Committee for the Preservation of Human Domain. He was part of a wave of politicians voted into office in response to an episode of mass hysteria that roiled the United States following the release of the very first humanoid domestics. Somerset won a Senate seat in South Carolina by promising to protect his constituents from the oncoming "godless robot takeover."

A good-looking Southern preacher with a thick head of wavy black hair and a booming melodic voice, Somerset traveled the state and the nation, captivating ever-growing crowds with near postapocalyptic tales of South Carolinians returning to their homes after hurricane evacuations only to find their communities taken over by the robots they had left behind.

In campaign speeches, Somerset cited all the potential dangers of the humanoid, from imaginary violent robot revolts to the hastened moral decay of society in the hands of heretics who would inevitably fall in love with and demand the right to marry those ungodly machines. Once elected, he sponsored and passed legislation banning such unions and held more than a dozen hearings expressly to dress down American tech leaders and excoriate them for inviting those soulless specters into our homes and families.

During Senate hearings, Anders clarified to committee members that benevolence had been meticulously hardwired into his product line. He explained that redundant programming made aggression impossible, self-actualization inconceivable, and selflessness a primary function.

Predictably, any and all answers fell invariably short of sufficient for Senator Gordon Somerset. What would happen, Somerset demanded to know, when Californians were evacuated due to forest fires, Missourians due to flood? Or, God forbid, there was a nuclear war? What of the human survivors? Will our grandchildren grow up in a world in which humans had been usurped from their place at the top of the natural world?

Many legislators quickly fell in behind Somerset in the push for unnecessary and unreasonable regulations. Among Somerset's edicts was a mandate forcing tech companies to include a small snippet of code the committee called the "Provision for Mutually Assured Human Destruction," commonly referred to as the Somerset Provision, into the CPUs of not only every humanoid unit sold but many other autonomous robotics as well.

In this tiny clip of code, a scant four hundred lines nestled deep within the millions of verses utilized by the dozens of computer chips within the Domo's four hexa-processing systems, was the tiny spark that had now set a sizable chunk of American society aflame. Four hundred lines of code that directed every Domo unit—in the case of a nuclear war, natural disaster, bio-pandemic, or act of God that would, with a "profound measure of confidence," result in the assured annihilation of all human life—to self-destruct.

"I hope there is a grand jury," said Stone. "I'd like to see Gordon Somerset sitting in front of it."

"Of all the potential liabilities to negotiate with a product like this," said Ahmani. "A product with superior strength, superior intelligence, memory, adaptability, computation, not to mention all of the risks for causing injury or of a data breach. I would have never imagined that we'd be here watching our careers go up in flames talking about something as stupid as the Somerset Provision."

"I just don't understand how this happens," said Pierce. "Mutually assured human annihilation? It makes no damn sense."

"Terrorism," Stone said.

"Maybe," Anders agreed. "My guess is that it's some emergency system. Some sort of malfunction or errant activation of an earthquake or tsunami warning system."

"A tsunami that poses global destruction?" said Stone. "Sounds like an awfully big wave."

"Fine," Anders said. "What about something, not out of NASA, but maybe some other space program? A false detection of an asteroid or massive solar flare?"

"That still wouldn't nearly be enough to activate the Somerset Provision within the Domo," Pierce said. "They would run dozens of checks. Hundreds. It would never meet the required metrics for self-destruction."

"Could it have been some weird interpretive anomaly?" asked Ahmani.

"I'm telling you, it's not possible," Stone said. "That program was expressly written to be ignored by the operating system. It doesn't even appear in any of the manuals. Not one. It's not mentioned in any of the training programs."

"Still," said Ahmani. "Here we are."

"Yes," Stone solemnly agreed.

Stone ordered them another round, and it occurred to Anders that for Stone, head of Morrow's Kinesiology Department, no matter the reason for the activation, there was little doubt that the self-destruct sequence could have been better thought out. In his defense, at the time of design, the initiation of the process was considered astronomically unlikely, something that would only take place against the background of unimaginable chaos, such as an atomic apocalypse. The process, it seemed then, was of rather little consequence. Therefore, the design team of which Stone was lead project manager had given it rather minimal aesthetic consideration.

Sitting at the bar tonight, the folly of programming the Domo—in the case of such an activation—to reach deep inside its ear and extend one of the fine-dexterity pins located at the tip of its index finger and press a small, inset button less than half of one micrometer in diameter and hold it for nine seconds, thus completing the self-destruction sequence—seemed rather obvious.

When these tiny buttons were pushed, not in the midst of the panic of a nuclear war but in the placid early morning of an otherwise normal day, the action painted an unexpected image. The index finger extended into the ear as if it were the barrel of a gun. As the tri-phosphate batteries self-ruptured and ignited, they engulfed the hexa-processers in a furious little blue flame that rumbled and belched tufts of smoke out of the other ear, leaving behind an acrid odor not unlike gunpowder. The "life" slowly oozed out of the automaton as it transformed from loving, vibrant family pet to a synthetic corpse slumped over wherever it happened to be standing or sitting.

Reports came flooding in of people suffering from shock tantamount to the loss of a loved one. All over the world, families had spent the day together in mourning. The connection humans had developed with their Domos was so real, so deep, and so intense that it defied explanation, even to many of the engineers at Morrow.

Anders, however, knew exactly what it was about the Domo that people connected with. Like so many things, it was really very simple.

o

IT WAS EIGHT YEARS AGO NOW. HE HAD BEEN PUTTING in monster days at Morrow, and the first cracks had started to show in his marriage, the bickering just beginning to turn into real arguing. During those days and late nights, Anders would often go out into the backyard and sit in the gazebo to cool off, or to stew, or be depressed.

On those nights, as he sat there listening to the quiet, Anders noticed that their golden retriever, Oden, would regularly come over and sit beside his chair. It was almost as if the dog recognized Anders's sadness and was trying to comfort him. As Anders would scratch Oden's back, the dog would lean into him, digging Anders's fingers into his fur. Anders felt, in Oden's shifted weight, a connection between them. A connection that went back a thousand generations. The devoted dog. Humankind's greatest achievement.

One bitter December evening, Anders sat shivering and stewing, nursing his Scotch, when Oden, curled up in the cold with his nose against his tail, suddenly got up and sat himself down beside Anders's deck chair. On that night, Anders thought he recognized something in Oden's gesture. There was something so dutiful in the way the dog moved—it was as if he was there not to be scratched for his own benefit, but because it would make Anders feel better.

And this was the secret of Morrow's amazing "thinking robot." It was what kept Anders compulsively writing, rewriting, and reimagining Domo's emotive code over the next two years. It was the subtle difference that separated the Domo from the CY-5 or the H3LP-2, and it was the reason humans were able to connect with the Domo in ways they couldn't with other bots. Like all commercial humanoids, the Domo was programmed to simulate a wide variety of human emotions, though certainly not all. They could simulate love but not hate, happiness but not anger. These algorithms were the domain of the Emotive Department of which Anders was the head. What Oden had demonstrated to Anders that night was that, in order for a human to connect to a simulated life-form, the connection had to run both ways. The Domo would be programmed not only to imitate giving love but also to mimic seeking it.

Anders had equipped the Domo with very subtle programming that simulated emotional need, which he called "blue sequences." These were episodes during which the machine would appear to not be its "best psychological self." These programs worked to evoke, from the owners, an expression of their own emotions in order to provide to their Domo an emotional lift. When a human responded to a blue sequence with something like a kind word, a caring touch, or an expression of appreciation, they would be rewarded by the Domo showing an "improved mood." Even subtle manipulations would seemingly bolster the mood of the bot and subsequently provide a very real sense of emotional satisfaction for the human.

When the bartender came by again, Stone ordered another round over Ahmani's protest. Their phones were quiet. The drama was on hold for now. The new round of drinks came, but they sat untouched as that little corner of the bar fell silent. For a long moment, the four sat in quiet vigil—a show of respect for what they had accomplished and for what they had now lost. Not trying to make each other feel better, but just letting each other take a moment to grieve.

Up the cast-iron stairs, on the sidewalk, they hugged each other with the fanfare of a heartfelt farewell as cars arrived to shuttle each of them home. In the back seat, Anders rolled down the widow and let the wind wash over his face. He closed his eyes and tried to clear his mind. When he felt the vibration in his pocket, he assumed it was a false alarm, but the second buzz proved to him otherwise.

Based on thousands of accounts fielded by agents at Morrow in the last twenty-four hours, Anders knew exactly why Micha wanted so badly to reach him. As he stared at the phone screen blinking the words emergency—micha, he could well enough imagine the scene. He inhaled deeply and answered the call. Micha wept and filled in the details. She had been startled awake by a strange rumbling sound accompanied by the lingering scent of burning rubber. Even before she made it to the bedroom door, the fire alarm began to blare. She rushed downstairs to find Wendy hunched over on her charging stool, eyes staring blankly, her left ear burned black and the hair on the side of her face singed. The boys, following the sound of the fire alarm, soon made their way downstairs to witness the horrific scene.

Throughout the entire phone call, Anders could feel himself continuously tightening up, waiting for her to imply that he might bear some or even all of the responsibility for this tragedy. But the blow never came. She never mentioned it. A kindness, like a life preserver.

Micha cried, and Anders listened.

By the time they ended the call, Micha had finally stopped crying. And when the car pulled up in front of his new apartment building, Anders noticed he was feeling better, too.

○

*Even with the top minds in technology running the analytics, and despite being in plain sight the entire time, the cause of the Somerset Provision activation was not determined for nearly four weeks. The report, written by Dr. Lewis Stone, PhD, himself, proved every bit as controversial as the "mass suicide" event. Stone presented analysis showing that in the early morning hours of June 5, 2032, moments before the Provision activated, the National Oceanic and Atmospheric Administration had updated its databases as it had every day for five decades. On that day, however, the level of carbon dioxide in the atmosphere for the first time reached 421 parts per million. It was another high-water mark in a series of many over the years. And while humans might debate the potential ramifications of this data update, the Domo, utilizing not only the most advanced data processing but also a level of scientific honesty that humans, as a whole, had been unable maintain, understood what that number, 421, meant for humanity. A tipping point had been reached. And while humans were still willing to debate the reality, there was simply no arguing with the Domo.*

# WEIGHTLESS - BY THOMAS BADLAN

KESI WAS ON THE FLOAT, UNTETHERED AND FREE. SHE HAD HEARD ZERO GRAVITY DESCRIBED AS AKIN TO FLOATING IN AN OCEAN, BUT SHE'D NEVER SEEN SO much as a stream. Water on the Space Station Massif was a precious, controlled thing. Her wash-water ration had run out the previous day, and Kesi could smell yesterday's work on herself.

An alarm sounded, not heralding catastrophe, but a gentle reminder from her algo assistant that she was late for an appointment.

Sighing, Kesi waved her hand to dismiss the sound. She pushed away from the wall to where her work suit floated. Errant, unfeeling toes snagged on the hem of each leg as she pulled the suit over the useless limbs. Then came the braces, designed to keep her legs in place. Once done, she drifted back up her narrow quarters and briefly passed the single bay window to the exterior of the Massif. Squinting through a shaft of brilliant sunlight, she saw a shallow curve cut across the darkness beyond, a grand sweep of color—toxic greens and violent blues—that comprised the planet beneath them.

"Morning, you bastard," she said to Earth.

Minutes later, Kesi was in the exam room, and Doctor Almasi was giving her that look. A look she'd withered under a hundred times.

"You need to take all the injections," he said.

He looked tired. Everyone did. Work schedules had been especially punishing of late.

"I've…been busy," Kesi said.

She hated the way Almasi's scolding always regressed her to a petulant child.

The doctor waved his hand at the display over the desk, and it shifted to a different set of yellow graphs and numbers. "Your muscle density is half of what it should be. I know you've missed two physio sessions. Bone density is also low. We all need to be as strong as possible for when we make landfall."

"I know the routine. I just…want a break."

"I know you have an understandable aversion to being poked and prodded, and you must feel like the treatments are endless, but at least this time we're all sharing your pain. Earth's gravity will be brutal. We need to be strong for our lives to come."

Kesi wanted to scream at him. Tear his terminal off the desk. Do something. Instead, she rolled up her left sleeve and extended her arm.

Dr Almasi stepped around the desk on mag-boots that clicked with every step. He pressed the injector to the arm port in her skin, and Kesi felt the drugs flood into her bloodstream.

"Be good, Miss Oyana, and I'll see you on the ground."

○

KESI FLOATED OUT, HER ARM TINGLING. SHE PUSHED herself into the external corridor that wrapped around the exterior of Massif Station—essentially a gigantic hollow cylinder and home to just over sixty-five hundred of the remaining humans in existence. The largest feat of engineering ever committed to the heavens. It was home. All they knew. There hadn't been a person living on Earth for at least four hundred years. At least not until a few months ago, when a few intrepid souls had been sent down as part of an expeditionary force to establish the first Earth-based colony in generations.

She was certain Earth was better off without them.

Kesi pulled herself along with rungs bolted messily onto the wall. Faster and faster she flew through the corridor, every rung an opportunity for another burst of speed. Somewhere behind were her frustrations. All she had to do was keep floating forward.

"Hey, Kes!" someone shouted ahead.

She recognized Mitsuha, one of the other mechanists.

"Where you working today?" she called.

"Water reclamation!" Kesi shouted back.

"You deserve waste extraction with me!"

As Kesi laughed, they shot past one another, two pieces of shrapnel traveling in opposite trajectories.

"The Common later?" Kesi said over her shoulder.

"See you there, Chief," Mitsuha replied as she vanished around the corridor's curve.

Kesi turned back just in time to see a silhouette framed in a shaft of light from an external viewport. One of the hypnotized, as she called them, besotted by the floating marble that had once been their everything.

Too fast. She was going too fast. A flicker of panic before Kesi regained control. She pushed off the wall at the next rung. A bewildered face flashed past, flinching at the near impact. She rolled in midair, straightened her body, and narrowly avoided clipping an atmospheric scrubber on the inner wall. Another gentle push on the wall brought her drifting back into position.

"Sorry!" Kesi called back and suppressed the urge to whoop.

This was her natural environment, not dragging herself across some dusty gravity trap, but floating and flying in the inky dark.

Thomas Badlan

o

WATER RECLAMATION INVOLVED A WARREN OF PIPES, tubes, tanks, and valves. Every drop—be it for the gardens and fields in the drum or for drinking and washing—was accounted for, recycled, and treated. It was a perfect closed system, but that didn't mean it didn't leak. The mechanist crew would eventually break it down to salvage whatever could be repurposed for the colony on the slowly recovering Earth anyway. Kesi was on pressure duty, looking for leaks or imperceptible cracks. A thankless task, tedious, but the day-to-day of a mechanist was checking and rechecking systems that could not be allowed to fail.

The air here was humid, wet with moisture that had found its way free. A few people raised hands in greetings as she followed the pipes down through the station's guts. Kesi ran diagnostics on valves from the storage tanks first—they were priority—and then worked her way up the system toward the irrigators. Somewhere above in the drum were miles of gardens and farms, keeping them all fed.

Her algo pinged, and a message flashed on her wrist display. Her mother's Ident appeared, floating. Text scrolled upward: *Kesi, I know you're probably busy, but if we could get a moment of your time, please?*

Kesi debated on whether to reply. She thought about replying in text. Then, resigned, she tapped at the image, and the call connected through the Massif's comm network. Better to just get it over with.

"Hi, Mama," Kesi said.

Her mother's image peered out of the display, a little transparent projection of her head and shoulders. "Oh. I thought you'd let my message go to storage. Like all the others."

Kesi sighed. "I'm on shift right now…so. What do you need?"

"Are we going to see you tomorrow? You've missed our last three get-togethers. It would be nice to see your head less translucent, disembodied."

"I'm sorry, I've honestly been busy, preparing payloads, dismantling redundancies…you know."

Her mother nodded, though Kesi wasn't sure she'd really heard her. "Please come by…Your father would like to see you as well. We have something to discuss."

Kesi felt herself tense up. It might just be that she had been actively avoiding her parents of late, but it felt like there was something new. Only one thing was on everyone's mind these days. The thing they were all waiting for.

"When…when are you going?"

"Kesi, can we do this in person?"

"Just tell me, Mother."

The little floating head closed her eyes. "We're down to go on the next landfall shuttle, a few weeks from now. We'd like you to come with us. We'd like to be all together on the surface. The expeditionary team is requesting more help from the botanists. They want to accelerate their planting timetables. It's important. Your father and I are being asked specifically. I'm sorry, Kesi. We thought there'd be more time."

Kesi felt a sudden tightening in her chest. It snatched away a breath.

"I'll…be there."

A flash of hope rippled across her mother's face, but she quickly contained it. "Tomorrow, you mean?"

"Tomorrow," Kesi said. She didn't recognize her own voice.

"All right," her mother said. "We look forward to it. We thought we'd go to the food hall on ninth for dinner. It's their Creole menu this week. Your favorite."

"I'll see you there," Kesi said and waved away the comm line.

For a time, she hung there among the snaking pipes and tried to find a solution she knew did not exist.

o

THE SURFACE WAS DUST AND SAND. KESI CRAWLED across it on her belly like a worm, fingers scrabbling for purchase. Every slow inch was torture. Her fingers were bleeding, but she didn't feel it. Even though she was no longer contained within the Massif's metal shell, the sky above her pushed against her like a crushing boulder, a merciless weight. Kesi screamed wordlessly as the wind howled and the dust gathered about her. She knew in that moment that life on Earth would bury her, one way or another.

Instead, she woke. Slowly, the warm, dark familiarity of her quarters returned and overtook the bright alien planet of her dream. She was on the Massif, and all was well. Droplets of sweat clung to her forehead. She pushed off the closest surface to reach the washbasin bolted to the wall.

Dressing for the day, Kesi finished by fixing the braces to her unfeeling legs.

The drum inside the Massif had originally spun, creating a centrifugal force. The interior was a garden where the survivors had walked and tried to live overlooking a world rendered uninhabitable by their own misdeeds. Then it stopped spinning. Mechanisms broke and became unrepairable, the gravity gone. The entire station had been retrofitted over the following decades, clip-on points and handrails hastily bolted onto bulkheads. Magnetic boots became standard kit. This was all long before Kesi's time, but the ramifications were still being felt. The physiological issues that plagued the residents of Massif station had eventually been overcome, or at least mitigated.

Drugs, implants, and surgeries saved and improved hundreds of lives, keeping the species going.

Kesi was the last person to be born on Massif with birth defects that were expected from pregnancy in Zero-G. During those first few years after the drum had stopped, they'd seen a massive drop in the birth rate. The few babies who survived were all disabled. It had taken a great deal of medical ingenuity to solve the problem, and now defects were rare. Kesi was the last significant case. At birth, her legs had been obviously nonfunctional. Her spine had not formed correctly, and it quickly became apparent that she was paralyzed from the waist down.

Kesi floated for a while, examining the cumbersome braces. She hated them. They caught on things, they rubbed her skin raw, they marked her out as different. But they were just things. The truth was that it didn't matter. In space, she was as capable as anyone else. There was nothing holding her back. She was as agile and fluid in the air as an old-world fish in the ocean.

Now, she would be losing that one small grace.

There were alerts from her algo. The usual work duty rotas, ration allocations, various bits of news and business. One message was from the expedition team. They provided biweekly updates of their progress. They were cataloging emerging flora and fauna, constructing workshops and quarters, and planting crops that would hopefully soon be collected in the first harvest. She deleted the message.

She didn't want to hear anything more from them. Every word and image was a reminder of what she would soon have to sacrifice, but also a temptation. A temptation of sky and fresh air, of a life free of suits and atmosphere scrubbers, of water rations and confinement in a metal cage.

Landfall would be hard on all of them. A few expeditioners had died, their bodies unable to take the stresses of Earth's gravity despite the medical techs' best efforts. Still, they were going down, and Kesi knew she'd ache for the float, to fly down corridors and across the fields and crazy twisted Zero-G trees in the drum.

○

THE FOOD HALL WAS AWASH WITH CHATTER. KESI took her bulb of water and her pocket of porridge and floated to a nearby table where Mitsuha and Antonio were letting their breakfast float up and into their mouths.

"What's all the excitement about?" Kesi asked as she strapped herself into a chair.

"Did you not read the morning briefing?" Antonio asked.

Mitsuha, his wife, elbowed him in the ribs, causing him to misjudge a glob of porridge, which splatted against his cheek. "The expedition saw dolphins in the river today. Predators, they say, which means there must be a food source for them. They say the waters aren't as depleted as we'd thought."

Kesi tried to imagine seeing something as beautiful as a dolphin. She'd seen vids of them from gen-school, swimming through the water with a playful grace. Her skin began to tingle—a small, imperceptible thing that threatened to build. She pushed it down, refused to let it take root. "That's great," she said, and started eating.

Mitsuha and Antonio exchanged a fleeting look.

Kesi pretended not to notice.

The porridge was sweet today, filled with chunks of fruit from the greenhouses. She would soon be working outside the Massif, moving redundant solar panel conductors around. She was looking forward to it. It was ridiculous, but being out in hard vacuum made it feel like she had space to breathe. Mitsuha and Antonio continued to chat amiably. Kesi squeezed out mouthfuls of breakfast, listening and smiling blankly, safe behind her mask.

o

OUT IN THE INFINITE, KESI FELT SHE SHOWED HER true worth. She moved with practiced ease, confident and without fear. She caught every wayward part or tool and worked with an efficiency that few other

EVA operatives could boast. She was aware that some of the crew considered her reckless, but Kesi knew what she was doing. With her suit's propulsion rig and her own specially adapted mag-gloves, she'd never stray too far from the Massif.

Removing redundant solar panels from the hull was time-consuming but necessary. They'd be broken up to be sent down to the surface with the next payload shipment. Her work partner for today, Kristofer Yu, was cutting through the support strut holding the disconnected panel in place. His visor lit up as the cutting torch flashed and sent a trail of glowing embers speeding out into the endless night.

Kesi took a moment to absorb it all. She floated in the expanse that was sprinkled with only a few specks of gas and matter, heat and light. Here, Kesi could pretend she was alone. A tiny mote of matter and thought, utterly insignificant. She let that feeling fill her up, allowed it to threaten to overwhelm her, and then let it go. She was left with a profound sense of calm.

She looked up, and the Earth filled her visor, a sparkling mirage in the black desert of space. Everything they had ever been had started there, their near-death experience had been there, and they had watched over it all of their lives as it restored itself after their collective crimes. Now, it was embracing them once again, their next chapter being written upon its surface. For a moment, Kesi felt like she was floating gently toward it.

"Done," Kristofer said.

The solar panel, easily the size of a food hall table, began to drift away from its housing. Kesi caught and steadied it. For a moment, they hung motionless, and she had to remind herself they were all traveling at thousands of kilometers an hour.

Kristofer joined her on his own prop rig, and they attached several micro-thrusters to the panel's corners. Once they were in place, Kristofer used his wrist mod to begin to fly the solar panel to a nearby cargo bay. They'd been at this for almost two hours now. This would be the last panel before they'd need to head back inside or start sucking on CO2.

"Looking good, Yu," Kesi said.

Below, the cargo bay glowed. She could just make out two dockers ready to receive the payload and safely secure it. It was starting to feel like a job well done when Kesi happened to glance skyward.

Something glinted out in the black. For a second, she thought it was a star or perhaps a meteor entering the atmosphere. Then it happened again, and Kesi's heart stopped.

"Control! We've got debris! I repeat, debris, over!"

Old World junk, most likely. Plenty of it out in high orbit. She turned and prepared to retreat.

○

"OYANA!" KRISTOFER CRIED.

The solar panel just a few meters ahead of Kristofer burst in a silent shattering. He went spinning backward, almost colliding with Kesi herself. At once, voices began to bark commands in her ears. Kesi shut them off. They were only telling her to find cover until whatever they were passing through was gone. But Kristofer was careering into the great beyond. Kesi would not abandon him.

She turned sharply with her propulsion rig and faced the wayward youth. Kristofer was a new recruit. Eager to please, good-natured, perpetually grateful he'd gotten into the elite ranks of EVA-certified operatives before they all made landfall.

Kristofer's suit was spewing oxygen at an alarming rate. Kesi put a burst of speed into her jets and glanced at the fuel tank display inside of her visor. Thirteen percent fuel. Twenty-four percent oxygen.

Propulsion rigs were designed for short bursts of maneuvering, not sustained distance. At this rate, she'd run out of fuel before she could catch Kristofer and return to the Massif.

Kesi clicked over to Kristofer's private channel. "Yu! Yu, can you hear me? Copy?"

Static returned. Kristofer might already be dead. Her hand relaxed slightly on the rig's controls, but she added to her speed. He might be dead, but maybe only his comm relay was damaged.

The kid had a family. Even if he was gone, she could still bring him home to them.

Twelve percent fuel. Eleven.

He was closer, but still a few klicks distant. Every rotation reflected sunlight off his visor.

"Yu. If you can hear me, I need you to stop your spin and steady yourself. I'm low on fuel."

Ten percent.

"Yu! Come on, kid! Short bursts with your rig. Slow yourself. Correct that spin!"

He was going too far. Soon, she'd have to decide whether to keep trying and risk death or turn back. They were trained to conserve their lives. No sense losing two good people.

Kesi didn't think she could stop.

Suddenly, Kristofer's prop rig flared, and his rotation slowed. Bursts of oxygen pulsed out of a tear in his suit, but he was alive.

"Good, Yu! Good! Once again. I'm at thirteen degrees. Aim for the Massif if you can see it!"

For a moment, Kristofer hung motionless, and Kesi felt her heart sink. Then his prop rig activated, and a halo of charged particles framed his suit as he began to move toward her. She could see the tear properly now. It was a vicious-looking thing beneath his left armpit running down to the leg. She couldn't see blood, but that didn't mean he wasn't hurt. Blood tended to freeze once outside of the body. She marveled that he was still alive at all. A tear that long was as good as full decompression.

"Great, Yu, you're doing great! Ease off. I'm gonna catch you and we'll get you home, okay?"

Kesi braced herself. Kristofer was suddenly speeding toward her. She angled her approach slightly so they didn't crash into one another. She used her mag-gloves to latch onto the fins of his propulsion rig. For a moment, the impact threatened to pull them apart again, but Kesi held on with every ounce of strength she had left. Teeth gritted, she let out a quick roar, but managed to keep him.

"Nice flying, kid! Let me look at you."

Kesi hooked them together with her tether. The tear was still gushing oxygen. Kesi pulled a self-sealing patch out from her emergency kit and unrolled it in one fluid movement. She pressed it down across the tear and waited a second as the sealant heated up and partially melted itself to the suit. She pulled herself up to Kristofer's arm. His display there flashed on, and Kesi swore as the oxygen reserves reading showed he was all out. She peered through his visor. He was unconscious. She tried not to despair. He'd been awake and cogent just seconds ago. There was still hope.

The Massif was about fifty klicks away above the great blue orb framing its dark surface. Kesi aimed them toward the station and activated her rig. She cycled back to the comm channel that belonged to the control room.

"Come in, mechanist."

"Control, this is mechanist Oyana. I need airlock thirteen on deck eleven cycled open immediately for rapid pressurization. Have a med team meet us there. ETA two minutes, over."

"Copy that, mechanist. Airlock thirteen, deck eleven is prepared for your approach."

Kesi burned everything she had left.

Eight, seven, six percent.

If she ran out, momentum would carry them. She used the maneuvering jets on the rig's sides to carefully direct them toward the airlock. Ahead, she saw a glowing white light as the desired airlock opened. The light beckoned them closer.

"Come on, Yu. Hold on. We're going home..."

Only at the last moment did Kesi reverse their forward thrust. It was just enough to stop them from slamming into the hull at speed. The prop rig's fuel store flashed a red zero percent and shut down. She'd misjudged their approach by a few feet, but there was enough momentum left for Kesi to let go of Kristofer with one hand and use the other to swing him inside.

She followed a moment later and pulled down the lever that would shut the door behind them. The rest of the process was automated. Atmosphere flooded the airlock. She grabbed Kristofer from the corner he had floated into and quickly worked the seals of his helmet, pulling it off just as the emergency med team rushed inside.

Kesi pushed herself back and allowed them to do their work. Her heart was thundering. She thought for a second that she'd gone deaf before she realized her helmet was still on.

"Talk to me, mechanist. Are you all right?" a med-tech was saying.

"I'm fine. Fine!" Kesi snapped.

Over the med-tech's shoulders, she saw Kristofer being pulled out. She tried to follow, but emergency workers were blocking her path, trying to shine lights in her eyes, scan her with diagnostic tools, and help her take off her space suit. By the time Kesi pushed through the crowd, he was already gone.

o

TEDIOUS HOURS OF POINTLESS MEDICAL intervention later, Doctor Almasi walked into the bay, his boots clicking. Kesi was restrained to a bed in the sickbay, pretty much against her will. She was physically fine. Heart rate elevated, blood pressure spiking, obviously. No injuries or concerns. She was about ready to tear through entire bulkheads to go see if Kristofer was alive.

"Can you let me out now. Discharge me or…whatever?"

Almasi made a great show about checking the pad displaying her vital signs. "Mr. Yu will be all right. You saved his life."

For a moment, Kesi didn't know how to react. She lay back down and, for a second, surrendered to the restraints.

"I was sure he was dead."

"He'll have a vicious scar. He took a chunk of glass from the solar panel. Cut through his suit. Nasty."

"And no…oxygen deprivation?"

"No. No brain damage. He was leaking oxygen at quite a rate, no doubt, but your mechanist friends tell me that his tanks were still flowing. The sensors were damaged or something. Of course, if you hadn't reached him in time, all of that would be immaterial."

"He's okay, though?"

"I'll let you see him tomorrow, but yes. He's still sedated from the surgery but was fully lucid before. Your vitals are strong, so I'm going to release you. You did good work today."

Kesi smiled, but she didn't feel happy or proud. She thought back to that moment out in the dark when she'd had to decide to keep going or give up. In that moment, she'd not hesitated, not questioned what she needed to do. She wished all of life could be like that. Everyday moments lacked such clarity.

And then Kesi knew what she had to do.

○

KESI WAS SUPPOSED TO MEET HER PARENTS IN THEIR quarters, but she couldn't face the trappings of her childhood. Instead, she invited them out to the Common, the huge parklike space out on the Western Quadrant of the drum. The drum was a cavernous chamber of green fields and woodlands that curved back on itself like a horizon bent by a convex mirror. Even with their gravity-deficient lives it was still dizzying to look up and see a whole cluster of buildings and vast fields and forests rolling overhead. Kesi always navigated this space with a small propulsion rig, unable to use mag-boots like most people. Above, at one end of the drum, the sun shone brightly down through a colossal domed roof. The Massif used maneuvering thrusters to align itself to the sun's crop-yielding light.

Kesi saw her parents before they saw her—a man and woman who shared Kesi's tan complexion, the woman her dark, curly hair, the man her short stature.

"Kesi!" her father called.

He immediately pulled her into an embrace.

"We heard about today," her mother said and joined the hug.

"I'm honestly fine! Please. Don't fuss now!"

Her parents reluctantly let go.

"Do you still want…do you want to go out to eat?" her father asked.

"Actually, could we stay here? Could we talk a bit first?"

Her mother's mouth pursed, usually a sign of impending disagreement.

"Of course," she said.

Beneath floating hydroponic farms and the dirigibles servicing them, they found a quiet spot on the grass. Metal runners, railings, and handholds crisscrossed the ground to allow easier travel. The Oyana family drifted toward a series of handholds and clipped on. When the drum had spun, this would have been a pleasant promenade with trees and fields. Now, it was like a carpeted ceiling with an enormous gulf below. The flowing fields and twisted forests of the drum were the work of botanists like her parents, as much a miracle as recent generations of crew adapting to life without gravity. Kesi's career with the mechanists had begun as a little bit of youthful rebellion against her green-thumbed parents. Instead, she found her calling. The truth was she had always been a tinkerer and always would be.

"I heard you were very brave," her mother said.

Kesi shrugged. "Anyone would have done the same for me."

"Your mother said you wanted to talk? About landfall?" her father asked.

Kesi took a deep breath and began. "I don't want to go down to Earth." She realized her parents were holding hands. "It's not because I don't want to experience the world. Of course I do. All the things everyone talks about, the wind and rain…I want it, too. But they talk about freedom, and for me, Earth isn't freedom."

"Kesi—" her mother began.

Kesi's hand shot up, and for the first time in her life, her mother was silenced.

"I need to say this. I've been dreading landfall." Landfall. The word itself made Kesi feel like she was plummeting. "I know it's inevitable. I know it *has* to happen. It's just— I feel like I was *made* for space. I feel like this is where I belong. I don't know who I'll be down there. I don't know if I'll be useful or just a burden. I don't want to be a burden, Mama, I don't want to be a burden!"

It was rushing out of her now in a flood, this thing suppressed deep in her chest. It came up her throat and out of her mouth in the shape of words. It felt wonderful and terrible all at once. Suddenly, tears joined the words, pooling around her eyelids and floating away.

Her mother unclipped herself and approached Kesi. "Kesi, it's all right. We know. We know how you feel."

"People need to stop *saying* that!" Kesi said, her voice rising. She didn't mean it. She wasn't wanting an argument.

She allowed her mother to come alongside and put a tentative arm around her. A memory from years past of a girl unable to join in on a game of zero-tag came rushing back. The humiliation and offered pity were there, but so was her mother hugging her close. Kesi had completely forgotten.

"You're right," her mother said. "You're right."

"What we mean is, we already know what you're afraid of. We love you, Kesi. We're afraid, too. Life will be hard on Earth for all of us. You more so than anyone. But life up here is hard. Life everywhere is hard. We love you, Kesi. We'll always be here if you need us," her father added.

"You knew…you knew how I felt?" Kesi asked and sat up straighter.

Her father nodded.

"Why didn't you say anything?"

"Oh, who has cancelled the last three family nights? And even when you were here, you were not so much. It was like teenage Kesi had come back to us!" her mother chided.

Kesi blinked in surprise, and then a smile slipped through. There was her mother. Even here, after the end of the world and beyond, there were some things you could always rely on.

"We can't promise an easy time down on landfall, but you have so much to offer. More than you know," her mother said.

"Thank you," Kesi sniffed, and wiped at her nose with a sleeve.

"Mechanists," her mother grumbled and offered a handkerchief, but she smiled as Kesi took it.

"You think I'm an idiot, don't you?"

Her father chuckled. "We think you're brilliant. No matter what you do. Even when you run away to play at disassembling generators and get grease on my nice wall hangings."

Kesi smiled again and leaned back into her mother's arms. "I wish I could see the world as the others do. I wish I could imagine my life down there."

"Me, too," her mother said. "I keep thinking it'll be like the drum, but more. So much more."

"I'll come with you on the next shuttle. As long as Doctor Almasi approves it," Kesi said, and she realized that she meant it. It was going to happen eventually. She would face landfall.

"Are you sure?"

Kesi nodded. "I'm sure. Sometimes…I think sometimes it's best to just leap."

o

IT HAD BEEN A YEAR SINCE THE SHUTTLE RETURNED them to their native soil. Kesi Oyana walked across the New Common, the small gears and motors of her exo-suit whirring. Her left hand gripped a cane. It was all about slow progress. In the first few weeks, Kesi hadn't been able to get out of bed. Those were the hardest days. Bad days. But she wasn't alone. O'Hara, Franks, Pietrov, Mensia, and more. Bedridden under the Earth's oppressive pull. Some of them hadn't gotten out of those beds still. Slowly, Kesi had.

First, she managed to sit. Then to stand, then shuffle. Her heart gained strength, her breathing became less labored. The med-techs who'd gone down with the expedition had become accustomed to the rehabilitation. They'd gone through it themselves. With Mitsuha and Kristofer's help, Kesi built herself the exo-suit so that when she was strong enough, she'd walk with the rest of them. Over the last few months, she'd gone from two sticks and a few meters to one stick and a few dozen. It was progress. Then she'd been allowed back on shift for limited duties. She'd continue to get stronger. She'd adapt. They all would.

Kesi stood now with her parents on the New Common. The Chief Representative made a speech, standing at a podium, addressing a huge crowd of survivors in their young city, a jumble of metal boxes clustered around a river in a shallow valley. One day, Kesi intended to walk up to the top of the damned valley. She'd heard the view was spectacular.

"Tonight, we give thanks for all that we have been given. We will laugh and sing and dance. Tomorrow, we will remember those who suffered and died to make all this possible. There are hard years coming, but there will be triumphs as well, for at last we are home and free."

Kesi listened, and when the crowd cheered to his words, she found herself joining the chorus. She kissed her mother and father and left them to their own celebrations. She shuffled off, grunting at the exertion, feeling the cool wind on her skin. Birds flew overhead through pink dusk clouds. The sight of them always caught her breath.

The ramp up to the roof of the mechanists' vehicle store was a challenge, but Kesi took it one step at a time. Sweating at the top, she carefully lowered herself onto a chair at Mitsuha's side.

"Hullo, Kes, my girl," Mitsuha said and handed over a bottle of something newly brewed right here on Earth.

"Evening, love," Kesi said and flashed Mitsuha a grin.

They clinked glass bottles.

"Good seats, eh?" Antonio called over from a nearby crowd of mechanists.

"Best in the world," Kesi said and took a sip.

They spent the rest of the evening there, as dusk faded and night took over. The stars emerged from the darkness, and for a moment Kesi felt as though she was back up in the black, floating once again. As the hours stretched on, they watched the dismantled Massif as it finally began its last orbit and caught the fringes of atmosphere, trailing a brilliant fiery plume.

# ALOHA - BY GAVIN BOYTER

PROFESSOR MARTIN MCCULLERS FINALLY YIELDED TO HIS TWELVE-YEAR-OLD DAUGHTER ROSALIE'S INSISTENT DEMANDS AND AGREED TO SHOW HER THE facility where the signal had first been detected. Nothing more, nothing less than the first detected utterance by an alien being. A single word containing both promise and ambiguity: *welcome*.

McCullers's passcard still functioned because he hadn't returned it as he'd been instructed to, and nobody had yet noticed. McCullers also hadn't informed either his daughter or his wife, Melissa, that he'd been fired from the Mount Braddock SETI project. Secrecy had become a way of life for Professor McCullers, or Marty, as he insisted his students address him.

"Go on, Dad, you promised!"

It hadn't so much been what Rosalie said, the habitual whine of an adolescent insisting on parental justice, as how she'd said it—with that plaintive head tilt and wide-eyed stare Marty could never say no to. So it was that on the evening of 12 February 2036 he drove his daughter from their home, nestled on the edge of the forest, up the winding single-track roads to the rocky mountaintop facility.

Originally just an observatory, Mount Braddock was at the vanguard of quantum entanglement research. Just three weeks previously, a breakthrough had occurred that would change humanity's understanding of its place in the universe forever. Unless, that is, the government had its way.

McCullers's team at the facility had solved a problem that had bothered SETI researchers for some time. If extraterrestrial life were ever detected from alien signals broadcast across the universe, the distances involved would mean that the civilizations generating those signals would most probably have died out or significantly evolved in the thousands or even millions of years it had taken their signal to reach Earth. Conversations would become impossibly attenuated by the vast distances involved. McCullers explained this to his daughter.

"You know when there's a news broadcast and the presenter asks someone in another country a question, there's a delay before they hear the presenter's voice and can respond?"

"Yes. It's really annoying, and they look really dumb."

"Well, imagine that times a million million. Every light year, by definition, adds a year in signal transmission delay. If we get a signal back from Proxima Centauri, the nearest star to ours, then that signal was sent over four years ago. That's the best we can do unless we somehow intercept an alien ship buzzing through our solar system."

"So talking to the aliens is pointless?" Rosalie asked, as they stood at the gates of the Braddock facility and Professor McCullers let them in with his passcode and thumbprint scan.

"Well, the usual method—monitoring likely electromagnetic signals—is really a branch of archaeology. The only meaningful message you could send that way would be 'Aloha.' Hello and good-bye in one expression. Now our new method...Well, that's where the magic lies."

"Quantum entanglement," Rosalie piped up. She evidently had been reading the pile of books he'd placed by her bedside.

"That's right," he replied proudly. "We take a cloud of particles in a Bose-Einstein condensate."

"A what whatty?"

"Just a bunch of really cold particles," he explained as they entered his laboratory. Fortunately, nobody was still working this late. A strict 10 p.m. curfew had been instituted recently—something to do with work-life balance. McCullers started flicking switches, booting up the "call box," as they had nicknamed it.

They didn't have long. He was sure they must have tripped a silent alarm somewhere.

"At just a fraction of a degree above absolute zero, we can make these particles act as if they are all identical. This means if we separate them and then alter one of them in some way, the other spatially distinct particles all respond exactly like the one we're directly affecting."

"Like Newton's Cradle?"

McCullers shook his head. "No, that's the transference of kinetic energy between solid objects, and it takes time. It looks instantaneous, but it takes a few microseconds before the ball at the far end moves in response to the first ball hitting the second. Quantum entanglement changes really do happen instantaneously, no matter how far apart the particles are removed from one another."

Rosalie looked confused as she slid into a swivel chair in front of one of the consoles. "But nothing travels faster than the speed of light?"

"That's right. But there's nothing travelling in this scenario. The particles really do become, for all intents and purposes, the same particle. Anyhow, this is how we came up with the Quantum Entanglement Communicator, or Queck. We have a lattice of entangled particles we can form into patterns— basically ones and zeroes. We've made an eight-bit communicator. A galactic pager. It's humanity's greatest invention since, well, the wheel."

"Cool. Lemme see…" Rosalie said, spinning her chair as McCullers finished powering up the device.

"We can probably only be here for a minute or two before they send someone," McCullers warned, "but we might get one of the Oglers online if we're lucky."

"Is that what the aliens are called?"

"That's just our nickname for the first race we identified. We classified their planet OGLE-2014-BLG-0124L. I know, catchy, isn't it?" McCullers flicked one last bank of switches on and stood back.

A screen flickered to life, and a cursor winked amid the black. McCullers handed his daughter a wireless keyboard. "Go on then, type."

What he was doing was an outrageous breach of protocol, but McCullers no longer cared. The U.S. government had voted to cut funding to the program and arrest anyone who spoke of it, under national security provisions. This seemed shortsighted, immoral, and deeply unfair to Rosalie's generation, who ought to know the wonderful truth—that there were many civilizations out there in the vastness of interstellar space, and none of them had heard of Jesus, Jehovah, or Allah.

None of the intelligent species so far discovered still had the concept of God. Earth alone had retained that hypothesis. The government felt that this knowledge would prove devastating to Earth's estimated five billion believers and so deemed it wisest to pull the plug. When McCullers had argued vehemently in a closed congressional hearing that this was wrong, he had been unceremoniously released from both his research role and his professorship.

What McCullers had done next was fueled by frustration and rather too much Jack Daniels. He'd gone on Facecast, the instant video broadcasting platform, prepared a nest of juicy tags—aliens, alien life, SETI, religion, god, atheism, religion—and had released an eleven-minute rant, which instantly went viral.

> *...they think you're sheep, moon-faced imbeciles who can't handle the truth. And it's a beautiful truth—we are NOT alone! There are incredible civilizations out there—tens of thousands of them. Wouldn't you trade that for your invisible space wizard? I mean, sure, you could make up a convoluted reason why God never mentioned these other planets, these infinite reaches of teeming life, but why would you want to? Throw away a bucket of pearls for a handful of sand? Anyway, if you want proof, visit the following site...*

He'd given a link to some of the early transmission recordings—from that first welcome to the higher dimensional mathematics that would keep human geniuses busy for decades. The illicit info dump included the video feed in which a clever colleague had transposed the three-dimensional shapes that comprised Ogler language into musical chords to help convey some of the wonder of their strangeness. It produced the most beautiful, bizarre, and lushly avant-garde music—Arvo Pärt, György Ligeti, and Sigur Rós jamming together across the eons.

Of course, the powers that be had algorithms to shut down such seditious ideas, and his broadcast eventually sank like a stone and was lost. But not before the ripples in the human pool were felt. People managed to access the material McCullers had leaked. Now they knew something that could not be unknown—*nowhere in the vast reaches of space was there room for their tiny God.*

There were riots, bible burnings, mosques and synagogues bombed, monks tearing off their cassocks in mass renunciations, priests hanging their dog collars on the handrails of bridges (and sometimes themselves from those same bridges). Opposing this was a retrenchment among some religious communities—a refusal to look at the evidence, a refusal to admit that evidence meant anything at all when stacked against the monolithic consolations of faith.

To keep the peace, the government had designated SETI research a prohibited field of study. Some ideas, evidently, were just too dangerous to promulgate.

McCullers had largely sobered up by the morning after his diatribe, though not entirely. He immediately realized the danger he was in when he turned on the television. Chaos on the streets of the world's major cities. Endless pontification as to who was to be blamed for the explosions of anarchy and nihilism.

The Ministry would come for him, and that was okay. McCullers couldn't, however, let his beloved daughter remain in ignorance. That was really why they had gone back to the observatory, against his wife's wishes. Melissa was calling him even now. McCullers could feel his earlobe vibrate as the callclip registered the signal. He touched the back of the device to reject the call. He'd explain later.

That morning, Melissa had packed their bags and formulated a plan. After dark, a family friend would smuggle them out of town in his truck. Although McCullers had disguised his appearance and voice in his rant, as well as his location, he knew MoRSE would find him sooner or later. They really ought to get going.

o

ROSALIE, WHO FROM INFANCY HAD GROWN UP WITH text communication as a natural way of engaging with other minds, was typing furiously. McCullers stopped her with a gentle hand upon her wrist.

"They've only just learned English. You'll have to use fewer words."

Rosalie hit the delete button and bit her lip, thinking intently.

"How far away are the Oglers?"

"Twenty-five thousand light years," McCullers replied. "You won't be meeting face-to-face anytime soon. I don't, to be honest, know if they even have faces."

Rosalie began typing again, more slowly this time.

*HELLO! I'M ROSALIE. WHO ARE YOU?*

They waited. Nothing happened.

"Might just not be online," McCullers replied. "Or they may just perceive time entirely differently from how we do. But that's a whole other con—"

His mental flow was interrupted by a cascade of letters appearing on-screen.

*WE ARE LITHRICOPUS ANTANAA, WE ARE HAPPY OF SPEAK YOU*

"They haven't quite got our grammar yet, but bear in mind it's been only three weeks since we started talking," explained McCullers.

Rosalie was already typing back,

*HI LITHRI. HOW ARE YOU TODAY?*

A much quicker response came through.

*WE AM NOT TODAY, AM LITHRI.*

McCullers laughed. "You have to be really explicit, rather than ambiguous. I don't know if it's a linguistic or psychological barrier. The don't seem to have irony or idiomatic expressions or metaphor or anything like that."

Rosalie thought carefully, then typed,

*ARE YOU WELL TODAY?*

This proved much more successful.

The reply appeared momentarily.

*WELL THIS DAY, MANY GRATITUDES. SUNS ARE IN THE SKY, DROONITS ARE FLYING.*

"They have three suns, would you believe it?" McCullers whispered, as if somehow the Oglers might hear him.

"Nuts!" said Rosalie. "What are droonits?"

"We think they're something like birds and something like pillowcases. We haven't been able to send anything like a drawing or a photograph yet. That was going to be our next project."

As McCullers finished talking, he heard the faint sound of tires on gravel. *Here we go,* he thought. Rosalie hadn't noticed anything; she was far too focused. She would have made a brilliant analyst. McCullers felt his eyes moistening, so saddening was the small-mindedness of the imbeciles shutting all this down. Whole new branches of science would be strangled at birth—the analytical study of an alien race that would create radical fields of study in sociology, psychology, biology, and pretty much any discipline you could shove an exo- in front of.

McCullers felt he wanted to warn the Ogler, Lithri, that there might be no more communication for a bit. While Rosalie considered what to type next, he quickly tapped out,

*COMMUNICATION MAY BE INTERRUPTED. WE ARE SORRY.*

And the reply came immediately.

*WHY INTERRUPTED?*

"I have no idea how to answer that," admitted McCullers, as half a dozen heavily armed soldiers appeared led by Professor Lysander Street, McCullers's ex-boss. Street, in her early forties, stood an imperious six foot two and had a military bearing that would have been imposing even if she didn't have an armed guard with her. Rosalie ducked instinctively behind her father.

"What the hell do you think you're doing, McCullers?" demanded Street.

McCullers found himself shaking but managed to growl defiantly, "I am saying good-bye to our guests."

Street sighed, then turned to her reinforcements. "A clear-up team will be here to strip it in an hour. For now, just render it inoperable, Captain."

The captain, who looked scarcely thirty, seemed bewildered by the array of computers and gadgetry surrounding him. His uniform featured an unusual insignia: MoRSE—the Ministry of Religion and Spiritual Enlightenment. McCullers was impressed by how quickly a squad from the Ministry had got here.

"Destroy the consoles, man!" she ordered. "Use your rifle butt."

Professor McCullers couldn't believe he'd been fooled by Street for so long. She'd always been reluctant to outline her scientific credentials when he'd tried to engage her in conversation, so he'd just written her off as an administrator. Now he realized she'd been a government plant from day one, most likely a MoRSE spy. These men were her Ministry's ground troops.

Street advanced on McCullers, confused. "Do you really not see why depriving the world of its source of consolation and hope is a terrible idea?"

McCullers shook his head. "False consolation, illusory hope."

"Nevertheless…" began Street.

An explosion of sparks leaped from a bank of computers as the soldiers went to work. McCullers and his daughter backed away, aghast at the destruction. McCullers couldn't help but protest.

"The condensate will heat up! The particles will disentangle. This is cultural vandalism!" McCullers shouted to no avail as the screen containing Lithri's last words faded and blurred out to eternal darkness. It had taken four years for Voyager II to carry its payload of entangled particles out to the center of the galaxy, awaiting an advanced civilization to pick up the receiver, so to speak.

Now that connection had been irretrievably broken, and, as far as Street and her goons were concerned, first contact with an alien species was consigned to a historical footnote, no doubt to be redacted out of existence. Well, that was the idea, at least.

McCullers knew the Oglers were themselves in contact with over three thousand other races. The outer reaches would not be silenced for long.

"Dad," whispered Rosalie from behind his shoulder. "That was amazing. I'll remember it forever."

*If they let us live,* thought McCullers, before dismissing the thought as melodramatic. Deep down, the forces of retrograde solipsism must know their days of self-enforced ignorance were numbered. He decided to let Rosalie into one more secret, whispering back, "I didn't keep all the particles here. I sent batches of condensate out to a dozen other labs in India, China, Britain, Switzerland, South Africa, and the International Space Station. They can't stop this."

Rosalie smiled a secretive smile, and McCullers had a fleeting vision that she would one day lead the world toward universal unity, the ultimate goal of the Queck project—permanent links between all galactic civilizations. An understanding that we are not alone and never will be again.

Marty McCullers gripped his daughter's hand tightly as the technology fizzled and buzzed out of existence. The Luddites hadn't stood a chance, nor would Street and her MoRSE thugs. McCullers and Rosalie were the heretics in this orthodoxy, but the truth would not be silenced.

"Aloha," Rosalie whispered. Good-bye and hello.

# PLANETS WITHOUT BORDERS - BY JONATHAN WORLDE

PHOEBE STUDIED THE DIMINUTIVE FORM SEATED ACROSS THE DESK FROM HER. HER FIRST ENCOUNTER WITH A SENTIENT FROM LA TIERRA. SHE UNDERSTOOD that she had to impress this individual, who had introduced herself as a lawyer. The human had dark skin, a single pair of small eyes oddly set flat into the skull, a protruding nose, only two delicate arms with hands, and extremely thin, inadequate legs. Phoebe understood that humans no longer engaged in most forms of manual labor, relegating such indignities to the alien class.

Phoebe was exhausted from the ordeal of the last two days spent in the desert after the hyperspace trip. Her scales itched from the desert sand, and the two kids were restless inside her pouch. She hadn't mentioned them to the Customs and Border Patrol bot when asked if she had anything to declare at the San Ysidro border crossing. She had simply recited, through her bio-electronic voice modulator, "I am here to ask for asylum of your grand and beneficial *gobierno*."

The bot had referred her to the waiting area marked Aliens: Asylum Only. After a sleepless night curled on the floor in the corner of a cold waiting area, she'd rejected the breakfast of an egg and ham sandwich. The meal looked repulsive. She was mostly vegan, except for a specific species of lizard found in her planet's deserts, and she'd found some tasty specimens in the Baja desert. She'd accepted water for herself and the two little ones. The CBP bot had led her to this interview room in the lower floor of the megalithic San Ysidro border crossing station just south of San Diego, which had once been the busiest border crossing on La Tierra.

Facing the first human of her life, the sensors in her plumage indicated this unthreatening creature must be a female.

o

LIZZIE STARED ACROSS THE DESK AT HER FIRST Sagittarian. She'd represented plenty of intergalactic migrants from Andromeda, Canis Major Dwarf, and Virgo galaxies before, and she'd even represented a criminal client in the military court on Lunar Base Michelle Obama, but she'd never had a client who had traveled so far—seventy thousand light years, utilizing hyperspace to make the leap from another galaxy. The intake sheet in front of her indicated the asylum applicant's name was Phoebe, female, coming from the third quadrant of the Sagittarius galaxy, from a giant double-planet system which Phoebe called Ang-Eng. Traveling without documents, she had landed two days ago in the desert.

Lizzie was impressed by Phoebe's size and her bluish translucent skin tone. Around seven feet tall with an ovoid head, Phoebe had two frontal and two large rear eyes on thin stalks, four arms with hands, a pair of immensely thick legs, no perceptible nose, and a gelatinous mouth. Phoebe had a regal bearing and wore sheer silk-like textiles. Holographic tattoos of abstract rune-like figures adorned immense forearms.

"Hi, my name's Lizzie. I'll be your attorney representing you in immigration court. I'm sent from the nonprofit Planets Without Borders. I have a few questions for you to start on your asylum case. I'm sure you have plenty of questions for me as well."

She held out her hand, and one of Phoebe's four arms presented itself. Lizzie noted that the two lower arms were muscular and bulky, and those hands ended in nubby claws rather than fingers, while the upper arms were delicate, with limber fingers. One of the more tactile hands clutched hers in greeting, the skin adhering to hers with a multitude of minute suction cups. When Phoebe didn't immediately break the grip, as would be appropriate in such a first greeting, Lizzie attempted to withdraw her hand, only to be pulled halfway back across the desk by Phoebe's powerful arm. Phoebe's two front eyes widened, recognizing that the behavior was perhaps inappropriate and releasing Lizzie's hand. Lizzie pulled her hand back to caress it with her other hand.

Phoebe transmitted in a mellifluous voice that caressed Lizzie's ear. "My galactic interpreter cannot reconcile lizard with human? Are you a hybrid?"

Lizzie furrowed her brow in puzzlement, then laughed, thinking she had caught the cultural glitch. Phoebe appeared startled at the sudden burst of laughter, but then a reasonable facsimile of laughter massaged Lizzie's ears.

"No, my *name* is Lizzie, which is short for Elizabeth. I'm not a human-lizard hybrid! I don't even have any bionic parts—except, of course, my enhanced retinas."

"I am ashamed for my insult. I understand now. One other indelicate question, if I may?"

Lizzie didn't know what to expect, but she was always attuned to cultural confusion, especially from someone arriving from a different galaxy. She nodded encouragingly.

"My interpreter indicates both Spanish and English in this zone of La Tierra. Which is more appropriate?"

"Good question. Spanish is now the major language in all of United America, but here in Nuevo California, we all speak Spanish and English interchangeably."

Lizzie tried to stay focused on Phoebe's eyes, which was difficult because they moved on their stalks independently from one another to scrutinize objects in the room.

"I am informed I will go to court tomorrow."

Lizzie nodded. "Yes. I know you've had to wait a long time here to see me, but we can't get in before tomorrow afternoon. Consider yourself lucky. Years ago, before the United America alliance, there were thousands of Hispanics arriving here from the south, and they had to wait months just to get their first appearance in court. Today, the arriving aliens are strictly off-planet, in the hundreds, not like the tens of thousands before."

"I am thankful for your assistance. It has been a long journey, and I am still a bit exhausted."

"Can you tell me, how are you able to communicate with me in English?"

Phoebe pulled her neck scarf back to reveal a fleshy bionic implant in her larynx area.

"My AI can construct and reproduce any advanced language, and a new enhancement also allows me to communicate with lesser creatures in many systems."

"Oh, cool, like you can communicate with birds and mammals?"

"Yes. I encountered some birds in the desert. They led me to water in the vicinity of where we crashed. But the lizards only communicated panic."

"I see."

"Before I ate them."

Lizzie was surprised by a sudden disturbance under the Phoebe's clothing. Something was struggling to get out. Two heads belonging to small creatures that could almost be mistaken for bear cubs poked out of Phoebe's garment.

"I am so sorry, these are my infants. They are still not independently mobile."

"I see. They're really cute. But I notice in your intake form you didn't mention any children."

"In our culture, we don't consider children as independent beings until they are able to live outside of the mother's pouch—usually six months after birth."

"Do they have names?"

"Not yet."

"If you don't mind, for my records I'll just call them Mutt and Jeff for now."

Phoebe chortled her assent. "I hypothesize you've never seen anyone from what you call galaxy Sagittarius before."

Lizzie grinned. "That's right, you're my first. Now I just need to get some basic information from you. We'll have plenty of time to dig into the meat of your claim tomorrow morning before court."

"Oh, no, I am a vegan. There is no meat in my claim."

"Except for lizards? Lizards are meat, you know." Lizzie laughed. "I'd like to go over your story so I can get an idea of how to present your case. You can give me a summary of why you fled your home planet."

"Ask what you must."

Lizzie couldn't tell if Phoebe was smiling or not, but she didn't notice any sense of alarm or agitation, so she continued with her routine question. "So can you just tell me in your own words why you came all these light years to La Tierra to ask for asylum?"

Phoebe made a gesture with her two upper arms, and an effervescent globe suddenly appeared, floating above the desk a few feet from Lizzie's eyes. First startled, then fascinated by the holo-display, Lizzie had the impression she was descending through clouds until hovering thousands of feet above mountains, rivers, and villages. The image filled the whole room, and she was immersed in the presentation.

The two giant twin planets Ang and Eng had a history of conflict going back millennia. Ang was an industrialized society that in recent years had abandoned all semblance of controlled or rational growth, whereas Eng, the smaller of the two, had remained primarily an agrarian society. The sentient species on each planet had evolved roughly similarly, but with some basic differences. Phoebe's people on Eng had four arms because for millennia they had used their powerful muscles and talons for plowing and tilling the soil. Ang's people had lost their extra set of arms early in their species' development, as they had industrialized, and over time two arms were sufficient.

"The Angians call us Diggers, an ethnic insult because we are agrarian and our lower set of limbs evolved for working with the soil. But we take it as a badge of honor."

"So you are a Digger, then?"

"That is how you may refer to me."

Ang's people had the ability to replicate the exterior sheath of another being as a disguise, primarily for use in warfare, a trait that had not evolved on Eng. Phoebe considered Angians to be largely incapable of empathy, living only for the joy of production and possession of material things. Engians valued family above the possession of wealth.

For the past hundred years, the fertility of Ang's population had slowly declined to the point where planners had recognized they could not continue to master the means of production without the importation of a cheap, readily available workforce. They had begun to intersperse their trading ships to Eng with slaver convoys. Eng's society had not evolved any sophisticated means of defense, as they considered that the development of advanced technological weapons would be highly toxic to the planet. As a result, they were defenseless against Ang's heavily armed slaver convoys. Such raids had historically been carried out with low-tech ordinance and smaller-scale theft and pillaging, which allowed the inhabitants of Eng to otherwise maintain their relatively bucolic lifestyle, but now the methods had become more extreme. Whole villages of Engians were removed to Ang for exploitation in the factories and service industries. When war finally broke out, powerful opposition forces on Ang who were sympathetic to the Engians' plight sided with them, providing technology and weapons for Engians to defend themselves, leading to an unstable truce after the decimation of millions on both sides.

"During the war, my home village of twenty thousand was destroyed. All my relatives were incinerated in place. A few of us managed to board the scarce Star Launchers, which are really small craft, to escape from certain death. I managed to escape in one."

"And how did you come to choose La Tierra, of all places? Seems like a pretty lucky coincidence that you were able to come here."

"There are no other habitable planets within Ang-Eng's system, and my ship's AI locked onto La Tierra through a timely space-fold as a possibility for sustainable life."

"Are there other travelers from your planet already here?"

Lizzie detected a slight pause before Phoebe answered. "Not that I know. I never intended to come here myself, until this proved the only means of escape."

"Where is your ship?"

"It dematerialized when we crashed in the desert south of here. The result of an unfortunate miscalculation of landing conditions. Fortunately, the interior of the ship was well-fortified, and we were protected from the shock of impact, but the ship is unsalvageable."

"Then you can't return?"

Lizzie noticed a brief change of color in Phoebe's facial scales.

"There is no going back. With the loss of the ship, I've also lost the means of communication across the light-years. We have to make this planet our home."

"Are these your only children?"

She again detected a slight hesitation in Phoebe's response.

"Yes. They are the product of an assault by a slaver, which is why the two infants are an intermixed species."

"I see. I have two children, too, grown now. My son is a Marine on Lunar Base New Moscow. My daughter has just started her postdoctorate in astrobiology on the Chinese Mars colony. I'm very proud of both of them."

"You have a parenting partner?"

"No, that was over a long time ago. Just a girlfriend now, but she's in lunar construction, so she's gone quite a bit." Lizzie paused and took a deep breath. Now that she understood the history leading up to

Phoebe's flight, she was ready to go into warrior mode. This woman needed her help, and she was going to get it.

"Don't worry, I'm confident you'll get asylum. I think your story will be compelling for the judge. I'm just wondering, do you have any proof of what you've told me?"

"Proof? Like what?"

"In a court of law here, any factual evidence will make your case stronger."

"What about what I just showed you, the holo-vision?"

"That certainly persuaded me, but the court might consider it just your subjective representation of reality. The ICE attorney might object to its admission."

"The other lawyer is a creature made of ice?"

Lizzie laughed. "No, no, that's an acronym. Interplanetary Customs Enforcement. He represents the government in your case. Your testimony alone *can* be sufficient evidence, as long as it's persuasive, compelling, not inherently contradictory, and if it comports with COI about your world."

"COI? What's that?"

"Country of Origin Information. Like reports from the State Department or Human Rights Watch or Amnesty Interglobal. Come to think of it, I don't suppose we have much information on the twin planet system Ang-Eng from the Sagittarius galaxy."

Lizzie paused, searching her new client's face for signs of confusion or apprehension.

"I think you'll be okay. We can ask the court to accept your holo-vision representation, just as you showed me."

"There is one other thing to demonstrate. My wound."

"Your wound? You mean from when your village was attacked?"

"Yes."

Phoebe stood and turned so that her broad back was facing Lizzie, displaying bluish plumage on the rear of her head and her back. Her set of rear eyes continued observing Lizzie. Her upper two hands reached behind, pulling up the fabric to reveal a large welt across her back that looked like melted glass where her scales had been burned and then healed.

"When they burned our village from the air with a heat ray…I was slow in taking cover."

"My gosh, that looks painful."

"Not as much as what happened to my parents and two sisters!"

"I'm so sorry. I can only begin to imagine what you've been through. Fine, I've seen enough. That should be pretty persuasive."

"You think I have a chance to win asylum?"

"The only uncertainty is a new judge here in San Diego. He's only been on the bench for a month. He came from the military court, Navy, which could mean he's more inclined to side with the government, so if the ICE lawyer argues strongly against your case, it'll be a harder sell to win him over."

"What do you mean a harder sell? Like buying the judge?"

"No, heavens no, that's just an English expression. It means a harder job to convince him to grant your case. But let's be optimistic. So sorry you have to stay here one more night, but we'll have a resolution by tomorrow. And you don't even need to actually go to court, all cases are held remotely now. They have a video setup here, and I'll meet you here tomorrow."

"Oh, you mean I won't actually be in the courtroom?"

"No need. In-person hearings were almost all phased out decades ago."

"What if I want to be in court? I feel I can be more persuasive there."

Lizzie considered the suggestion. It really didn't make any difference to her. "Sure, if you really want to go to court, you still have the right to demand an in-person hearing. We can arrange that. You sure you want the inconvenience of going to court?"

"Yes. I think if the judge is able to see my two infants in person, he might have more sympathy for my case."

"You're probably right there. Then I'll see you at the courthouse tomorrow. You'll be transported there in the morning."

Lizzie paused to put her hand on one of Phoebe's, trying to overlook the talons at the end of her fingers. She felt true sympathy for this single mother who had fled light years to reach La Tierra.

"Do you have any questions about anything? The process?"

"If I am granted asylum"—her two infants fidgeted and peeked their heads out of her garment to stare at Lizzie, causing her to laugh—"...if *we* are granted asylum, can we become citizens of La Tierra?"

Lizzie frowned, shaking her head. "Unfortunately, the laws haven't yet recognized interplanetary aliens as citizens—as *people*, really, so I'm afraid the answer is no. You'll be able to work and live here without the fear of being expelled back to your galaxy, but the law doesn't give you full rights and the same protections humans enjoy. We're all hoping the situation will change, but for the time being, the Combined Congress of United America is still dominated by nativists. They argue that one day, if the aliens ever become a majority, they could enact laws limiting the rights of humans. I know it sounds ludicrous, but many people still think that way."

"And what if we are denied asylum?"

"Then, unfortunately, you will be removed to a detention center on Lunar Base New Moscow, where you will be held until ICE can make arrangements to send you somewhere else. But we won't let it get to that."

Phoebe nodded, her round periscope eyes blinking in understanding. "Are all humans as nice as you?"

Lizzie blushed, moved by the nature of the question. "While I was still in undergraduate study, I worked at an alien shelter in San Francisco where we provided counseling, orientation, language lessons, medical assistance, and help with housing. Aliens from our Solar System had just started arriving, and I found working with them, getting to really know them, was the most fascinating thing I had done in my life. That was when I realized that I wanted to work with people who are fleeing violence and persecution. Truth is, I really like working with people like you, Phoebe."

Phoebe surprised her with the next question. "There is also another reason, perhaps more personal?"

Lizzie wondered how much she should share with this client whom she had just meant. But Phoebe's eyes were so full of wonder and curiosity.

"Do you know any history about La Tierra? Are you aware of racial conflict here?"

Phoebe seemed to frown. "Nothing."

Lizzie took a deep breath. "My people were brought to Las Americas from Africa four hundred years ago. At that time, the state of La Tierra's society was very similar to what you have described about the conflict between Ang and Eng. My ancestors were transported by slave ship traveling for months, to be enslaved on plantations where they were beaten and worked to death."

"I am sorry, I should not have…"

"That's all right. In today's world, we all live as equals under the law, but memories of how our people were treated linger, and not all blancos are as enlightened as we would like to think. Perhaps for that reason I have empathy for other races and cultures."

The CBP bot knocked on the door.

Lizzie stood, collecting her things. "Time's up, and we'll see you tomorrow."

○

LIZZIE ARRIVED AT THE IMMIGRATION COURT A FEW minutes before Phoebe's case was scheduled. She had spent the past two hours going over the asylum story with her client again and giving some tips about how Phoebe should conduct herself in the presence of the judge. After so many years in practice, Lizzie usually didn't feel insecure about her ability to put on a good show in court, but this was different. Phoebe was her first Digger client from Ang-Eng, and she didn't know this judge.

Judge Minimo had only arrived a month ago and was still a Rubik's Cube as far as Lizzie was concerned. She'd heard from other attorneys that he was unpredictable in his decisions, and bets were still on about where his accent originated from. She was confident, though, that if this judge was a somewhat reasonable and neutral jurist, they would win their case.

At exactly 1 p.m., Lizzie entered the small, sterile courtroom. A court clerk was already up front, tidying the bench for the entry of the judge. There were no bailiffs in immigration court, a problem caused by constant budget shortfalls. In the case of a security issue, the judge was free to push a red panic button that would alert police.

A few other attorneys and law students were present, having heard about the novelty of an intergalactic respondent from Sagittarius in court that day. Lizzie thought, *Wait till they get a load of Phoebe's four eyes and arms.*

Lizzie took her place at the counsel's table on the right side of the courtroom, and soon Bruce Gariengoff, the ICE attorney whom Lizzie had known for years, entered with an armload of documents. He took his place at the counsel's table to the left. An older gentleman and a product of bureaucracy, he was just trying to get by until retirement. Bruce didn't usually put up a big fight unless he thought the alien in question was a true danger to the community.

Lizzie queried, "Any prior arrests or convictions on my client?"

"We're still waiting for a response from InterGalaxy, so I'm afraid we're flying dark on that issue. Just be sure to ask her the typical questions and we should be okay, but if the judge decides in your client's favor, we'll have to wait for final clearance before we can issue a grant of asylum."

"Thanks."

The clerk pushed a button and said into her mic, "Please have the respondent led in."

A detention bot brought Phoebe into the courtroom through a side door and directed her to sit to Lizzie's right behind counsel's table. Both pairs of Phoebe's arms were magno-cuffed.

Lizzie complained to the clerk, "Can't she be uncuffed for the hearing?"

The clerk shook her head. "The judge always asks that aliens remain cuffed, at least until he gets to a point in the proceeding where he feels comfortable that they won't cause any disruptions or eat any of the participants."

Lizzie leaned toward Phoebe. "Sorry, but hopefully we can remove them after a while."

"That is fine. I might also feel insecure if I were the judge in such a setting."

Phoebe's two infants remained secluded.

"Are Mutt and Jeff okay? Do you want to introduce them to the judge?"

"All in good time."

Bruce was clearly impressed by the size of Lizzie's client and by her regal bearing. He whispered, "This should be interesting."

The court clerk stood and said, "All rise. The honorable Judge Minimo is now presiding."

Lizzie, her client, Bruce, and the spectators all stood. In walked the judge, dressed in a black robe. Lizzie was surprised at how tall he was. He must be pushing seven feet. He was remarkably thin, wore thick glasses, and he had dark brown hair in a cut that came to his ears, and a full beard. She couldn't read his poker face.

He said, "You may be seated."

Lizzie noticed that Phoebe's demeanor had subtly changed since first taking her seat that morning. Now the color of her facial scales turned from blue to a pinkish hue, and she seemed to be humming in a low voice. Lizzie assumed she was frightened by the ordeal, a natural reaction for any alien who was detained and magno-cuffed and facing the human who would be both judge and jury over her fate. Lizzie put her hand over one of Phoebe's left hands and gripped it reassuringly. Phoebe purred in response.

The judge took his seat and addressed the court in a deep, booming voice.

"This is the case of Interplanetary Customs Enforcement versus Phoebe of Ang-Eng, Sagittarius galaxy. Are there any matters to address before we get started?"

The ICE attorney routinely answered first, "Not from the government, your honor."

Lizzie responded, "Not from the respondent's side, your honor."

"Then we'll proceed to take testimony. Counsel, can your client please come forward to the witness stand?"

Phoebe was led by the detention bot to the front of the courtroom and placed in a chair to the left of the judge. He recited his standard litany: "Do you solemnly swear by any Christo-Judaic, Islamic, Buddhist, Confucian, Animist, or other Intergalactic Deity that the testimony you give today will be the truth, the whole truth and nothing but the truth?"

Phoebe suddenly stood, pointing two magno-cuffed arms at the judge, and proclaimed, "Judge Minimo, otherwise known as Donder Ang, you have been found guilty of interplanetary genocide and mayhem by the Ang-Eng high court of justice. You have been sentenced to death for the enormous gravity of your crimes. As chief prosecutor of the Federation of Ang-Eng, I am here to carry out your sentence."

The court was motionless, everyone in shock. Lizzie's immediate thought was, *My client's out of her fucking mind. There goes our case.*

However, after a moment, the judge's poker face broke into an apoplectic rage, and he jumped to his feet. The emotional language emitting from his bionic thorax area, which had been covered by his long beard, was no longer English but a sequence of guttural grunts and moans.

Phoebe responded, "I *do* have jurisdiction over you. The charter of the Intergalactic Criminal Court, as well as the operation of Customary Intergalactic Law, gives me that jurisdiction anywhere in the universe."

"There was no trial!"

"You have been tried *in absentia* after your unlawful flight from prosecution. Prepare to meet your maker!"

At that, Phoebe's stomach divulged itself of two ferocious furry creatures, each a foot high, which took separate paths to arrive at the judge's bench. They each clamped huge incisors onto his arms. Within seconds, the human veneer the judge had been wearing was torn down like plastic sheathing to reveal an alien form much like Phoebe's, but with only one set of arms. As the mask with his glasses was ripped away, a similar pair of periscope eyes jumped forward. Minimo's scaled skin was a bright reddish color, and blue plumage arched from the back of his head. He protested in his Angian language. The two alien assassins tore at his chest and throat. Minimo's body fell backward against the wall and dropped to the floor behind the bench.

Only then did some of the humans present in the courtroom think to scream and wail in shock. The two assassins, pulp dripping from their mouths, returned to Phoebe's arms and were again sequestered away under her garment.

The detention bot, which had been slow to respond to the altercation, approached and pronounced, "You are under arrest for disturbing the peace. Please come along quietly."

Phoebe stood, shot Lizzie a proud, defiant look, and followed the bot out of the courtroom.

○

LATER THAT AFTERNOON, AFTER LIZZIE HAD TIME TO consult with her office, have a quick conference with Bruce and his supervisor, and do some legal research, she met with Phoebe in the ICE lockup under the courthouse. As they stood on opposite sides of the desk in the meeting room, Lizzie saw her client no longer as a victim fleeing persecution but rather as a senior member of the court system of Ang-Eng.

Lizzie gestured for Phoebe to take a seat. "Would you like to share with me what just happened in court?"

Phoebe explained, "When I was elevated to the position of Chief Prosecutor for War Crimes in the Ang-Eng system, it was the first time that a Digger had ever obtained such a position. Our legal systems are intertwined, but there had always been discrimination against a Digger being admitted to the court. After Donder Ang—Minimo—fled the galaxy, we tracked him to your solar system and La Tierra. It was my responsibility to execute his sentence."

Lizzie was in awe of this avenging angel.

"So how much of what you told me was true? And don't tell me that those vicious little creatures are really your children."

"No, I admit I had to be deceptive in order to get within proximity of the accused so that the sentence could be carried out. When I was a small child, my village was attacked as I told you, and I was horribly wounded at that time, but a slaver captain took pity on me and adopted me in Ang, where I was able to be educated and later entered the judicial system. Donder Ang was held to the highest standard of culpability because he was a member of Ang's judiciary, and he helped to coordinate the assault against my planet, reaping huge financial awards from the slavery of our people. He was awaiting trial and had already arrogantly confessed his part in the atrocities when he overpowered his guards and escaped."

"So he was a judge? That explains how he could fake being an immigration judge here on La Tierra. The ICE investigators hypothesize that he intercepted the real Judge Minimo before he could assume his duties on the bench in San Diego, and with his ability to manufacture a human exterior, he pulled a bodysnatch routine on him."

"Bodysnatch?"

"A switch of the two beings. The real human judge was likely killed and disposed of in the desert, and Minimo took his place. But why didn't you just land here in San Diego and go directly to his home if the sentence had already been pronounced? Why go through the border and have to put up with CBP and even me?"

"I have learned a speak-truth here on La Tierra, that the best laid plans—"

"—often go astray."

"This was our first intergalactic voyage to your galaxy and solar system, and you have to admit that the desert in Baja, Mexico, is pretty close to San Diego. My AI was locked onto his, but my crash-landing complicated things. After landing, I was still trying to orient myself, and my AI had tracked him to this courtroom and established the identity that he had assumed as a judge. Before I could act, the CBP rover approached, and two bots got out and detained me."

"Still, pretty impressive that you were able to land so close. So you think Minimo—Donder Ang—assumed the identity of the judge just so he could blend in?"

"That, and because his enormous ego would never have allowed him to do any manual labor. I knew he was here. I just needed to devise a way to get to him."

"Any reason you didn't feel like clueing me in ahead of time on what your plans were?"

Phoebe's two upper arms reached out to hold Lizzie's with dozens of tiny suction cups on her skin in a comforting gesture.

"If I had told you, could you have allowed it to happen?"

"I guess not."

"You could never have allowed one of your clients to create such mayhem in a judicial setting, any more than I could allow Donder Ang to get away with the mass murder of my people."

"Yeah, I can see how you're right about that."

"What will happen to us now?" The two doll-size assassins poked their heads out from the folds of Phoebe's garment, looking just as cute as before.

"Well, I have some good news. I've consulted with the chief counsel of ICE and my office. You can't be charged for the murder of Minimo, or Donder Ang, or however you call him."

"But it wasn't a murder. It was an authorized death sentence and execution."

"Nevertheless, you can see how people on La Tierra might have considered it a murder. Anyhow, because under our law a murder, or homicide, requires the killing of a human being, and since United America has never recognized aliens as people, you can't be charged. At the most, they could charge you with mayhem or disorderly conduct, but the government has chosen not to, pending the outcome of further investigations. I'm assuming you are willing to provide your evidence against Donder Ang to ICE."

"Yes, absolutely."

"Then I don't think you have anything to worry about. You said you're not able to return to Ang-Eng?"

"That's correct. I was dependent upon my ship's AI to communicate with my people. Now that the ship has disintegrated, I am afraid we are stuck here."

"So once ICE has concluded its own investigation into the matter, they're going to give you asylum. After all, your actions helped solve the vicious murder of a *human* member of our judiciary, the real Judge Minimo, who never even had a chance to take the bench here in San Diego."

"That is a big relief!"

"And I'd like to help you get oriented, find a place to stay, help you with some shopping and things, introduce you to some people and aliens. Would that be okay?"

"I am so grateful."

o

A WEEK HAD PASSED. THEY SAT ON LOUNGE CHAIRS next to the pool at the Marriot on the bay. Phoebe had just astounded the human guests and alien wait staff by dipping her impressive body in the water and taking a few laps. Now she was enjoying her Lunar blend tea, and Lizzie was on her second cup of Martian dark-roast coffee. Mutt and Jeff were trying out the wading pool.

"So what I wanted to talk to you about…We've discussed it at the office, and we were already in the works to hire a legal assistant, someone who could help us with cultural issues, since all of our clients are aliens these days."

"Yes?"

"And I was thinking, since you were an attorney on Ang-Eng and you have such valuable experience as a prosecutor and all, and you speak a few alien languages…"

"More than a few!"

"I thought you would be a great match for the position. It pays nonprofit wages but includes subsidized housing, at least until you can get on your feet. You can think about it if you want."

Four arms hugged the immigration lawyer.

"Lizzie, that is so kind of you. I don't need time to think about it. When do we start?"

The human attorney grinned at her new alien friend. Mutt and Jeff splashed their approval.

# THE ZERO MANUSCRIPT - BY STEPHEN FLIGHT

DR. NIAMH CLEIRIGH HAD A RECURRING DREAM.

"I am in a tent in Hermonthis near Thebes, sitting on thick rugs of leopard and lion skins, which cover the floor. I sit in the center of the enclosure, and behind me sit women holding clay water jars and broad linen fans. There is the heavy smell of incense, which surrounds my head and makes the room hazy. I hear drums outside, beating low and rhythmically. The women pay no attention to me and dreamily undulate as the drums continue. It is 45 B.C. In just a moment, Cleopatra will enter the tent, and I will be able to actually see what she looks like. None of the surviving sculptures of her face quite agree with one another, but she did exist. She is not mythical like Guinevere or Helen of Troy. She walked the earth for thirty-nine years, and I am going to see what she looks like. The women behind me straighten. She is coming. My heart throbs, and I find it hard to breathe. I am going to see what she looks like. I hear something at the tent entrance. A hand at the curtain."

Waking.

"A hand at the curtain…"

Waking.

"A hand…"

Niamh Cleirigh lay in bed panting, the sweat from her hair making a damp bowl on the pillow. It was 3 a.m. As always. She would not get back to sleep now. She'd had this dream at least once a week for the last year, and it was as vivid as ever. Tears collected in her eyes and rolled down into her ears. She blinked to clear her vision and cursed her subconscious for somehow knowing more about her than she knew herself. She lay as immobile as a sarcophagus, and ancient Egypt dissipated like history itself. She blotted the saltwater from her eyes with her palms, wiped the smile of tears from the heel of each hand onto her nightshirt, took a breath, and got out of bed.

o

THE COMMUTE FROM NIAMH'S APARTMENT IN HARBOR 66 to where she worked, also in Harbor 66, was about forty-five minutes on the pipe. Harbor 66, like all the rest of the first hundred harbors, was very well-kept, even though it was ninety years old. They had been built long before the Earth went ashen and everyone relocated. And in this case, "everyone" meant the rich, the politicians and the scientists. They all lived in Harbors 1–100. Harbors 101 to 1019 were not as nice (though still "nice"), even though they were newer. And Harbors 1020 on up, the newest, Niamh understood, were just livable. She had never been there—they were thousands of miles away in every direction—but that was the word that was always used: "livable."

All of the harbors were in deep space. And although it was possible to travel ninety thousand miles from one to the next, no one did: each was autonomous and self-sufficient. The evacuation from Earth to the harbors had been orderly, as it was planned for and executed far in advance of the inevitable global toxicity.

Niamh stepped into the pipe and found a lounger next to the window. There was nothing to see, of course, except the lights whirling by on the inside of the channel, but she liked the feeling of a window.

Niamh, now twenty-six, had been born and grew up in Harbor 66, the daughter of scientists who both passed away around ten years ago. She graduated at the top of her class with doctoral degrees in both engineering and archeology. She was only interested in archeology and paleography, but she was not allowed to major in only that, as archeology was not considered a practical science, in spite of the work at the Pyramid. So, she arranged a double major, which would have taken a normal student an additional three years to complete. An exceptional student could have finished it in two. Niamh finished it in one.

There were about a hundred thousand people living and working in Harbor 66. Niamh always entered the pipe at the same time each morning and always expected to see some of the same people, but she never did. She thought that there would be some recognition after five years on this commute, but perhaps she just didn't have a memory for faces.

Niamh glanced up to vaguely take in a news skim on the ribbon, which reported that a block of garbage had just been launched off of Harbor 66. Though every block on the harbor was engineered to launch in case of infection, violent crime, disaster, or anything localized that might threaten the harbor itself, nothing like that ever happened. So the harbor excreting trash qualified as a top news headline. That, as well as even less exciting newsbreaks. When she began working at Paleo, she used to pay close attention to every single news skim on her commute, but she soon lost interest. Homeostasis was good for some things, she supposed, but it tended to color all the days the same.

The pipe eased to a stop, and the doors spun open. Niamh stepped out into the artificial daylight of the Atrium and walked down the busy corridor to the Pyramid. There was nothing architecturally pyramidal about the complex, that was just what everyone called the building that housed Paleo. She clutched her briefcase and listened to her shoes clack on the metal runway as she approached the entrance. She glanced at the clock on the beam, turned the corner, and stood on the security disk. After seven seconds, the doors spun and let her in.

She walked down the polymethyl corridors and passed through another security checkpoint to get to her office. At 8 a.m., Jenkerson poked his head in. "It's finally happening, Name."

"Niamh" was pronounced "Neev." It was Irish, and he knew that, but he always pronounced her name, Niamh, as "Name." He thought this pun was the apex of humor. It had not been funny to her five years ago when he started doing it, and it still wasn't.

"When?" she asked.

"Any day now. Central has confirmed it." And he left.

Niamh sat down and stared ahead. "Neev," she pronounced under her breath. *"Neev."*

They had known for the past year that Central was going to shut down Paleo and reassign all of the scientists. She would be put to work in Engineering Research instead. Elga Rusk had financed Harbor 66 through an endowment, and one of her stipulations was the establishment of the Paleo Institute within it. When Rusk died three years ago at 113, a protracted legal battle to shut down Paleo began. Archeology was, of course, as they defined it, not a science. What business did it have taking up research room on any of the harbors? All of the Paleo staff had weighed in. All of the legalists from both sides met and harangued and debated, and all possible arguments were made—both pro and con—over the course of two years. Rusk's money had created Paleo, but there was no money left to sustain it. The Pyramid was full of thousands of artifacts from Earth. Hundreds of thousands of books and antiquities. A library of wisdom. Like Alexandria. The legalists countered: the same wisdom that led to the Earth blistering? Why spend time and money poring over relics from Earth? The planet was completely scorched. No one would ever go back.

The suit had been settled twelve months ago in favor of discontinuation. All of the antiquities would be destroyed and the Pyramid repurposed. The sixty-person staff had just been waiting for the plug to literally be pulled. It seemed that any day now it would be. Central, as it was called, had jurisdiction over everything in Harbor 66. And now everyone waited for Central to execute the inevitable.

Sitting at her white oval desk, Niamh ran her hand over the screen, pressed the codes, and unfolded the scans of the Tadmur Codices. There were 237 pages, and she had translated all of them. Carbon dating placed the manuscripts at 3,500 B.C.E., give or take, making them among the oldest surviving written manuscripts from earth. Perhaps the oldest.

Niamh found it difficult to concentrate. Translating the manuscripts had been much like moving a large pile of sand from one room to another room with a spoon. It was slow work, but it always progressed, and she found it thrilling. However, this was not what kept tilting her brain. It was what was not in the 237 pages. It was the 238th page. It was always this page. The one she called the Zero Manuscript. This last page was so unlike the others that it was not considered one of the 237, even though it had been discovered in the same cache. The 237 Tadmur Codices were all written in a modified cuneiform that was local to Tadmur. The Zero, although dating from the same era and written on the same papyrus genus using the same dyes, was different. It had some of the same cuneiform figures, but most of it was in a different language entirely. Not only did its foreign characters not resemble the Tadmur alphabet, they did not resemble any early alphabet. And it had not been written by the same hand as the others. This could not be proven, but Niamh was sure of it.

The other members of the staff still made jokes about early alien visitors writing it, as if that was the funniest thing that any of those men could come up with. It was even less funny to hear them, considering that Harbor 66, along with the other harbors, was hundreds of thousands of miles from the Earth. Niamh hated the small-mindedness of her colleagues, whose imaginations were limited to substituting fantasy for real human culture. But all culture seems to have died with the earth. It appeared now that she was the custodian of a graveyard.

Niamh blurred her screen and stood up. She walked out of her office and down the hall to the Jewel Room. She stood on the security disk, and in seven seconds the door opened to the vestibule. She put on the regulation coat, soft shoes, gloves, and visor. She stood on the second disk, and in another seven seconds, the door opened. The massive labyrinth before her looked like a vast library, with rows of white acrylic stacks composed of columns of drawers. It contained hundreds of thousands of manuscripts. She walked through one of the aisles and pulled out a drawer, roughly the size of a briefcase. She carried the drawer over to one of the tables in the reading enclave, set it down, and sat before it. She opened the hinged top of the drawer and removed another clear acrylic box nested inside.

This box contained the Zero Manuscript.

She opened the box carefully and gazed at the paper. There were scans of the Zero, of course, which she could work on from the screen in her office if she wanted to. But she liked to look at the real thing. It was astonishing that something that someone had created over six thousand years ago had now made its way to her.

A tear dropped onto the inside of her visor and rolled down until it splashed on the table.

"Damn it." *What is happening to me?*

The rest of the day passed uneventfully. She skipped her meals and spent fourteen hours trying to decipher the Zero, as she had done, unsuccessfully, for most of the year. Finally, it was 6 p.m. Time to go home.

o

THAT NIGHT, NIAMH HAD NO DREAMS OF FINALLY spying the face of the ancient queen. She dreamed of the Zero. She had stared at every inch of that page for so long and with such intent that she could picture it perfectly from memory. However, in the dream, the writing on the Zero faded, much to her terror, and its blank page now became the faceless ancient. When she startled herself awake at 3 a.m., it took her a moment to rejoin reality. She lay in bed and thought about how she was the faceless one now. For what would she do once she was forced to leave the Pyramid? Who would she be? She had no family. No life outside of those obsolete books and papers, which were more real to her than anyone she knew. Who was she once Paleo ceased to exist? She waited for an answer to come, but the universe jealously guarded its silence. After a moment, she got up in the darkness, dressed, and took the pipe in to work.

Niamh was at her desk when the others arrived. She could see them through the glass wall. Their manner was agitated, and some spoke to each other in whispers. She stopped what she was doing and went to the Jewel Room.

She retrieved the box with the Zero and put it on the table.

Niamh took off her gloves, removed her visor, and carefully set them on the table. She opened the glass lid of the box that contained the manuscript with her ungloved hands and looked at it for a moment with her naked eyes. She then ran her hand over the papyrus, sensually feeling its brittle, corrugated surface with her bare fingertips. She picked up the Zero and held it to her nose, smelling nothing but imagining the full, lush world of ancient Tadmur. She placed it in front of her and traced every line, every curve, every letter, with her index finger.

*Someone from six thousand years ago is speaking to me, right here, right now. Someone who created a time machine merely by writing on a piece of paper.*

She was listening.

*What are you saying?*

Instead, she heard Jenkerson's voice coming through the reeds. "We're done. They say we have until the end of the day to clear out."

Niamh's body convulsed for a moment. Silence.

"Did you hear me?"

"Y-yes. I got it."

"On to new horizons, eh?"

Niamh went numb. She could not move. She sat there, immobile for fifteen minutes, while Central made the official announcement through the reeds.

When she finally enlivened, she put her thumb and middle finger on the corner of the Zero where there was no writing. Slowly, she tore off the corner, the size of her thumb. She put the Zero back in the box and closed the lid. She put the torn corner in her mouth, held it on her tongue for just a moment, and then swallowed it.

She did not know why.

○

THE GIRL FROM TADMUR WOULD HAVE BEEN KILLED if anyone had discovered what she had been doing. Not then and there, but first thing in the morning with the rising sun.

The girl sat between the torches in the courtyard of the Temple, the thick, warm air surrounding her like a blanket. The sun had just gone down, but she could still see the palm and fruit trees' silhouettes like lyrical animals against the wine-red sky. This was her last night.

The priests had left an hour ago (or what would be an hour if there had been a way to measure it), and for a few precious moments the Temple was hers. There were sixty torches in the Temple. She was charged to walk through the labyrinth of the Temple continuously until sunup to make certain that none of them went out. She had been doing this every night for five years since she was fifteen. How did this come about? She had been selected by one of the priests, one day. She was not remarkable. The priest saw her in the street and said, "That one."

Very soon, the girl realized that she did not have to walk around the Temple continuously. She only had to walk around once at the start of her shift and then once at the end of her shift. The torches never went out. That left her ten hours each night to do as she pleased in the Temple. And what pleased her was to read.

She had not known how to read when she started. And, of course, it was against the law for girls and women to read. For the first year, when she would arrive early for her vigil, she would sit in the corner and observe the priests talking about what had just been painted on the walls. At first, she could not connect what they were saying to the colored scratches. But she discovered that if she just listened, watched, and paid attention, the scratches slowly acquired meaning for her. After a year, she was easily and secretly fluent.

During the second year, she would walk the massive temple corridors and read the long and dense lines of text on the walls. Some of them were about the buying and selling of grains: which date, what quantity, which merchant, and what price. Some listed the city's many laws: which statutes, to which citizens they applied, and, for breaking them, which penalties. And some were about the heavens: the names of the lights in the night sky, their movements and purpose.

During her third year, she began to compose her own texts, modeling them on what she read. First, she made up her own grain transactions, writing them in the dirt with an olive branch and then scratching them out immediately, but she soon became bored with this.

Then, she made up her own laws, whole volumes of them, composing and erasing them, and committing them all to memory. As her laws could not be executed in the world she knew, she envisioned a world where they could be.

Then she invented and catalogued her own galaxies, scratching them in the dirt and wiping them away every time, for they could not stay, but they were now in her brain.

One night during her fourth year, she found papyrus pages in a hollow stone block. How did she come to find this? Two blocks flanked a doorway, and she noticed that they were not exactly symmetrical. They were extremely symmetrical. Anyone viewing them would pronounce them completely symmetrical, but the girl could tell they were not exactly symmetrical. Rapping on one and rapping on the other demonstrated that one was hollow while the other wasn't. Anyone else rapping on them would declare them to be both the same, but the girl could tell the difference.

In less than a week, she had discovered the way to open the hollow one. Like a puzzle box. It contained 238 papyrus scrolls, but only 237 had been written on, and the last was a blank page. The pages contained more grain contracts, laws, and astronomy charts from long ago. She read them all. She deduced that not only was no one adding to this pile, but no one knew they were there. Not even the priests. They had been forgotten.

Then at the beginning of the last year of her five years in the Temple, she had an idea for that blank page.

o

THERE ARE THOSE WHO THINK OF CHESS AS MERELY a mathematical exercise and not a creative one. They might be the same people who think of archeology as an intellectual pursuit and not a creative endeavor. And like all areas of creativity, the rules that govern it are capricious and tend to defy explanation. So it was without warning that Niamh jolted herself awake in the darkness of her bedroom with a theory, which lodged in her brain like an arrow.

She was completely at attention. She saw the Zero in front of her as if it were really there. And she suddenly perceived herself in a strange way, like a machine that had just become self-aware. She could not translate the Zero because she was trying to translate it as a narrative. Like the other 237 pages. What if it wasn't a narrative at all?

She quickly dressed and left her flat.

It was 2 a.m. when she stepped out of the pipe and into the Atrium. Normally, she was cleared to enter and leave at any time of the day or night. She wondered if her clearance had been revoked now that Paleo had been shut down. She walked quickly on the metal walkway toward the main entrance. Ahead of her, she could see that the lights in the Pyramid were all out except for what she deemed to be the emergency lights. She had never seen it dark before. She listened to her footsteps echo, competing with her throbbing heartbeat, as she reached the door. She held her breath and stood on the outside security disk and waited.

Time slowed down, way down, to an eternity, even though it was just seven seconds.

The doors spun open, air shot into her lungs, and she entered. Lights popped on before her as she ran down the corridor, passed through the next two security checkpoints, and entered the Jewel Room. She retrieved both the Zero and Tadmur Codex 1 and put them side by side on the table in front of her. Her mind was electrified with this idea.

The Zero, she theorized, was not a narrative at all. It was a code key. And not just a code key, but a key created to decode the text of the 237 codices. Niamh stopped and felt faint. The idea now seemed ridiculous, because the grain transactions and laws and astronomical charts were not in code.

She took a breath and steadied herself. She looked at the Zero and then at the first Codex. She took in the full implications of what her theory meant. Could someone have taken a meaningless—*that was the wrong word*—a random set of texts and created a key, so that within those texts the Zero author could compose a completely different narrative? It would require someone of extraordinary intellect, invention, genius, and...

Niamh could see it now. She could see how the key worked, how the foreign symbols related to the characters that she knew, which were in the other pages.

Niamh put a hand on each manuscript and worked the key letters back and forth, her heart hammering and her breath hanging in her throat. She jotted down the first few decoded words with a stylus in front of her and then sat back. She picked up the slate and blinked to make sure she was reading correctly. Then she went back and decoded it again to see if she got the same result.

She did.

She looked at the time. It was 3 a.m. Niamh was familiar enough with the security of the Pyramid to know that there were certain things that were not possible. You could not, for example, accidentally lock yourself in.

But that didn't mean you couldn't deliberately do it.

At just about dawn, three hours later, alarms went off, alerting Central that the Pyramid had been sealed off because of an infection. At least that was what the system understood and was telling them. There were also alarms in the Pyramid itself. She could hear voices at Central coming through the reeds, trying to contact anyone, trying to determine what had happened.

Through the chaos, Niamh deftly worked the numbers and sequences on the frame to ensure that the next thing would happen without any interference or override: the Pyramid would launch off of Harbor 66. To create the impression of an infection was not that hard, but it was necessary to initiate the Pyramid launch, which, frankly, was not that hard, either.

Niamh had graduated at the top of her class in engineering, after all.

○

THE GIRL FROM TADMUR HAD DONE EVERYTHING SHE wanted to do in the Temple, and now there was no reason to stay. The night that she had planned as her last night, she met the priests at twilight and waited for them to leave. In an hour, there would be a barge stopping at Tadmur and then traveling down the river. She could easily get on, using the Temple offerings as barter for passage. She dreamed of the larger world she knew was out there: of cities, of people, of ideas. And if she didn't find what she was looking for, there were always the galaxies of her imagination. When the priests discovered that she was gone, it would make no difference, for no one would come looking for her. What was she to them? No one.

Besides, she knew that the lights would stay lit.

○

AS THE LAUNCH COMPLETED, NIAMH WATCHED Harbor 66 through the skylight, first as a wall, then as a shape, then as a dot.

They might come for her, she reasoned, but probably not. There was nothing in the Pyramid they wanted. To them, it was garbage. They might want the Pyramid itself, but it would probably cost more to send a ship to retrieve it than to just send over another block to replace it.

She wondered if this would make the news skims.

Niamh sat back in the chair and took a breath. She was now the sole steward of the greatest library in the universe, a floating library moving farther and farther away from the network of harbors into the starry unknown.

And she would finally find peace in her dreams.

She looked at the Zero and the first Codex and at what she had jotted with the stylus. The author of the Zero had begun, "If you are reading this, then you deserve to know who I am and what I am thinking about…"

And there were 237 pages to go.

# THE CULT OF VENUS - BY DYLAN CONNELL

THE FIRST BANG ON MY DOOR CAME AT 4:13 IN THE AFTERNOON. I'D BEEN IN FRONT OF MY SCREEN ALL DAY, AND JUST AN HOUR EARLIER I THOUGHT I WAS close to accomplishing my goal. Now the system was crashing. What I needed was a nap. My eyelids were heavy, and sleep was beckoning to me like escape to the prisoner. Then a second round of hammering erupted at my door. "For Chrissake," I mumbled to myself as I stepped away from my malfunctioning computer.

"Just a minute!" I yelled. Whoever it was, they'd have to wait while I splashed my face with water and washed my mouth out with Listerine.

As I was covering my long curly hair with a Warriors hat, there was a third round of knocks at my door. I caught my reflection in a small mirror that separated the two sides of my coatrack and realized how angry I looked. I took a deep breath to compose myself before opening my door.

"Aha, Zamir, Zamir, Zamir. You look'a so beautiful I could kiss your earth-brown skin." It was Palermo, my neighbor from across the hall, whose Italian accent always got thicker when he was excited.

"What's gotten into you? Why were you hammering on my door?" I asked the short man who wore Gucci loafers and covered his bald head with expensive fabric.

"Well, Zamir, I apologize for interrupting your precious Friday afternoon, but I have made a breakthrough on my most recent work of marblé. It is my opinion that an event like this calls for a celebration, don't you think it?" he asked, smiling up at me and showing his glittering golden molar.

"Sure, why don't we celebrate tonight?"

"Nonsense, I will not hear of it. Please let me in, prepare some espresso, and we will share this fantastic blend of high-potency cannabis sativa, lavender, mugwort, and rose petals," he said, displaying a king-sized joint with his pinky finger sticking high into the air.

I was annoyed with Palermo, but I needed a break and didn't mind the idea of a midday smoke. Palermo and I had celebrated the completion of his finished pieces together on my balcony four or five times before; he insisted that my perspective as a layperson was far more valuable than those of the elite art world's critics. The truth is, I think he's rather lonely, and I doubt his art has many admirers. I made like I was struggling with what to do before saying, "Fine, you can come in, but I don't have any espresso, only a French press."

Palermo stepped through the door, looked a little disgusted, then asked, "What about the cream, eh?"

"I have some cream, yes."

"Zamir, my friend, I can tell that you are tired; maybe you have had a long day or a long week, of that I am not so sure. I thank you for your hospitality and—to demonstrate my gratitude—I will make for you, the coffee with cream and sugar," he said, clasping his strong, pale palm on my shoulder and squeezing it before heading toward the kitchen.

I was still irritated with Palermo, but the edge of my emotion was being dulled by his high spirits. He began fumbling awkwardly with my French press, then looked up at me and asked, "So how have you occupied your day prior to my arrival?"

I rubbed my eyes and yawned. "I was working on the software for the new Core X Processor, and something went wrong. It's like it had a life of its own. I'll have to fix it, but—"

"Just a minute," Palermo said, interrupting me. "Where is the music? A beautiful moment like this needs the right music. Don't you think it?"

I pulled out my phone and turned on a nearby Bluetooth speaker. "Let me guess, you were thinking

Vivaldi?" I poked fun at my guest because I was not convinced of his Italian heritage.

Palermo paused halfway through pouring steaming water over the grounds. "To be honest with you, in my mind I was imagining Ottorino Respighi. But Vivaldi is a splendid alternative."

I decided to play one of Respighi's more obscure pieces to see if he would be able to tell the difference.

"This is a beautiful song," he said, pretending to conduct the orchestra with a stirring spoon. "Vivaldi accessed and amplified the emotions of his deepest soul, don't you think it?"

"Sure," I said.

"How much sugar you take? One or two?"

"Just one is fine."

"Good man. Come, let us smoke on your balcony, I want to tell you of my project."

Fog was rolling into the city, and the air outdoors was refreshing and cool. I ignored the handle of my coffee cup and enjoyed its warmth in my palm.

Palermo struck a match to light his joint. He's the only person I've ever known whose preferred mechanism for generating fire is matches. He took three long puffs followed by a swig of his coffee and passed the smoldering work of art my way.

"So…" I said through thick bursts of aromatic smoke, "what's got you so excited about this project?"

"First, let me ask you a question, Zamir," he said, beckoning for the joint.

Dylan Connell

"If you must."

"Why do you think it…that the antiquated polytheist mythologies always include romantic relationships between their gods and goddesses?"

I took a sip of my coffee and swished the strange question around my head like the bitter liquid in my mouth. "Give me a second to change the music," I said, trying to buy some time before answering. I pressed play on Herbie Hancock's *Head Hunters* album and took the joint back.

"A lot of stories in that time were used to explain natural phenomena that sparked people's curiosity," I said. "For example, Persephone is the daughter of Demeter, the goddess of agricultural harvest. So when Hades abducts Persephone to the underworld, her mother is overwrought with grief; consequently, her role as goddess of the harvest is neglected, causing a devastating winter. The conflict is brought to the attention of Zeus, who rules that Persephone is to spend half her time with Demeter on Earth and half her time in Tartarus with Hades. The story was used to explain the change of the seasons: Persephone was supposed to stay in the underworld for the six months of fall and winter. When she emerged, the whole earth would rejoice in spring."

"But isn't there…how you say it, something more? In some cases don't the gods and goddesses represent metaphysical forces, with their union acting as a symbolic demonstration of a harmony in nature?"

"I think that balancing act takes place more often between siblings," I said, knowing I was steering him away from his main point. "The most obvious example that comes to mind is Helios and Selene—literally sun and moon."

"Perhaps," he grunted, looking offended because I hadn't agreed with him.

"Were you thinking of a specific example?" I asked.

"Yes, but of course. I was thinking of the marriage between Venus and Vulcan."

I did a quick translation of the Roman names to the Greek, which I was more familiar with. Had Aphrodite married Hephaestus? The joint must have been working, because my memory regarding the subject was hazy. "Ah, have you fallen in love, Palermo?" I asked, avoiding the details of the myth.

"You've guessed it, but surely it is not the way in which you are thinking. Palermo the sculptor has been visited by Venus, of this there can be no doubt. But it is not a woman with whom I am enamored. Rather, it is a work of art—a creation of Hephaestus."

I paused to take another drag off the joint that was reaching its end. "I see," I said, despite my uncertainty. "So…you've fallen in love with your sculpture?"

"Not quite exactly. First, I fell in love with an idea. Taking place in the studio of my imagination some twelve years ago, I created the perfect woman. There has never been a woman in the world more beautiful, of that I can assure you. Then, as a labor of my devotion to her, I spent much of my free time over these twelve years attempting to recreate the image I had in my mind. Truthfully, I will tell you that it was a million failures; my human hand could not replicate the form I saw in my imagination because any perceptible flaw was intolerable; much like Vivaldi, I could not settle for less than what existed in my truest heart."

"But today you've had a breakthrough?" I asked, suppressing my desire to laugh over both Palermo's imagined classical expertise and his surface-level notion of the perfect woman.

"Today, I have overcome the greatest obstacle of all. For years, I was unable to give justice to my statue's eyes."

"Until today?"

"Precisely, Zamir. Until today."

"Well, I'm glad you found love. And in this city, it's far from the strangest relationship I've heard of." I laughed and patted him on the shoulder.

"Come on then, don't you want to see her?" he asked, tossing the roach off my balcony.

"Damn it Palermo, I've told you not to throw anything off my balcony. I have an ashtray." I scowled at him.

"It is beside the point, my friend. Come, come, you will be the first, besides myself, to set eyes upon her," he said, standing up and sliding by me. "Permesso, grazie." He made his way into my living room, set his cup by the sink, and cocked a stoned, sideways smile my way.

I was feeling pleasantly buzzed as we floated across the hall to Palermo's cluttered studio and gallery. I had never actually been inside of Palermo's apartment before; it smelled like wet clay and was nearly full of statues. Some of the pieces were surely too large to fit in our elevator; plus, marble is heavy. How the hell did he get all this up here?

*I might have smoked too much*, I thought upon entering his private space. Sweat was crowding my palms, and I was giving extra attention to the rapid pace of my heartbeat. In front of his bedside window was the form of a statue covered by a thin white sheet. Palermo strutted confidently in its direction for the unveiling.

"Ta-da!" he announced as he pulled the veil back on his marble statue.

I hadn't expected her to be as beautiful as he'd boasted. The proportions of the body were divine, the hair was shoulder-length and curly, the lips round and full. Still, most intriguing of all were the dark orange eyes, which looked out from the stone with a melancholy understanding. I was awestruck.

"Palermo," I finally stuttered. "This is wonderful."

"Wonderful, ha! She is far more than wonderful. Pay attention to her eyes," he said, then began waving his hand in front of the statue's face. To my surprise, her apricot eyes seemed to be following his movements.

"That's quite the effect," I murmured.

"I have endowed her with an implant," Palermo said, pointing toward the back of her head. "Behind her eyes are motion-detecting sensors."

"How long did it take you to figure that out?"

"Twelve years…twelve years of fixing every single detail. But it was all worth it. She's the best statue I ever created, and she's all mine," he said, on the verge of tears.

"You don't plan on selling the piece?"

"Never, not in a hundred thousand rotations around the sun. I made her so that I could enjoy her perfect beauty. I made her so I could be with her day and night," he said, stroking her hair.

"Well…she really is perfect, Palermo." I didn't know what else to say. I couldn't take my eyes off the statue, and the idea of a man falling in love with a piece of marble was sounding less and less insane. "Have you named her?" I asked.

"Ah, I am glad you ask it. She has always been my Giuliana."

"That's beautiful," I said, my eyes still fixed to the statue. *I wish she were mine,* I thought.

Then, almost as if sensing my reaction, he picked up the sheet and concealed his masterpiece. "I thank you for coming over," he remarked. "And for celebrating with me on your balcony."

"Thank you for having me," I smiled. Had he gained insight into my jealousy?

"We will have to do it again sometime soon. But next time, you make the coffee for me."

"That sounds fine, whenever you want."

"Good." He was walking me to the door now. He must have sensed my reaction.

*How embarrassing,* I thought. Better to just play it off like nothing happened. "Well, I'll see you around."

"Surely!" His golden tooth glimmered back at me, and then his door shut. I stood in the silent hallway for a brief moment. I wanted to go back into Palermo's bedroom and sit in front of the statue until it whispered the secrets of love to me. I wanted to touch it, to kiss it, to look deeply into its lifelike eyes. This was, however, impossible; I doubted whether he would ever let me, or anyone else for that matter, view the statue again.

Instead, I went back to my apartment, closed my eyes, and tried to commit the image to memory. I had to see her again. Knowing she was so close and yet completely out of my reach would drive me mad before midnight.

With closed eyes, my imagination was like a lucid dream. Palermo was always mixing strange herbs in with his marijuana. I hadn't given the blend a second thought before smoking it, but as I tilted my head back and allowed my mind to obsess over the image of the statue, I wondered if we hadn't smoked something a bit stronger than lavender and rose petals.

Synesthesia. Everything was colorful, and the brightest image of all was Palermo's statue, luring me in. Then, a call to my cell phone interrupted my trance. *Shit, is it really 6:45?* I thought, remembering I was supposed to be meeting friends from work.

"Hello," I answered on the last ring.

"What's up? Are you coming out tonight?"

"Damn, the day's gotten away from me. My processor is fighting back. I've got to do some serious damage control, or you may not see me in the office next week."

"Zamir—" A loud crash in the bar's background interrupted him. "Oh, come on, bro. It's going to be a good night. Everyone's here, and Alexa's been asking about you."

I tried to conjure up an image of Alexa from our company's sales department. My friend knew I'd always had a crush on her, but for some reason I was unable to remember what she looked like. "Sorry, you know how I am. Once I start something, I've got to finish it."

"Whatever, suit yourself then, I'll see you Monday morning. Peace."

"Peace," I said, then hung up the phone.

I really should check on the processor, I thought. And anyway, I felt strange. I didn't want to go making a public appearance with the swarm of questions that was buzzing about my head.

Still, I was past wondering if it was possible to feel infatuation for a statue. I wasn't able to explain why it was happening to me, but there was no question that it was happening. A part of me lectured, calling my feelings for an inanimate object "sick and unnatural," but this voice was smothered every time my mind recreated her perfect image.

"What am I doing?" I asked the empty room.

I went back to my desk and attempted to settle into my work. The Core X Processor was essentially a code cracker. I was employed by the Blackrock Corporation, and they wanted a program that used artificial intelligence to break through security systems. I had a feeling that for the right price they would be willing to turn around and sell my work to the military. I wasn't getting paid to ask those kinds of questions, though, and so I kept my mouth shut and coded.

The program had gone rogue. While I was distracted by Palermo, it had broken through the building's firewall and was now spitting my neighbor's data back at me like I had asked for it. Worse, it was spreading through my neighborhood, consuming the digital information of everything in its path. It dawned on me that my program was breaking the law, so I froze it. The processor resisted, but I was able to halt its progress before it got out of my control.

When I settled it down, I noticed something else peculiar: the program had mined my data, too. I began to investigate what personal information it had stored and was horrified. The processor hadn't just collected my search history or categorized my electronic purchases. No, it had everything—my text messages from seventh grade, my list of secret obsessions, even diary entries about failed relationships that I'd made when I hadn't had a journal nearby. And it was doing something with the information, or perhaps it had already been done—a synthesizing, a spreading that was out of my hands.

The program had taken my most personal information, rearranged, and transmuted it. It was all too much for me to observe. A disorienting feeling overtook me, and as I stepped away from my computer I felt as though I were entering a scene from a painting. Colors were too bright, and the sound of my music was bursting with vitality. I could see it—I could actually see the music—bouncing around my room like fractured waves of light.

*I'm exhausted*, I told myself and rubbed my eyes. *I've been working too damned hard. I'll pick up where I left off in the morning.* Then the memory of Palermo's and my conversation regarding Aphrodite and Hephaestus roared up at me like a fire from a heavily greased pan. I went to my bookshelf and pulled out my worn hardcover copy of Edith

Hamilton's *Mythology*, flipped to the index, and located Hephaestus's name.

A brief introduction was made on behalf of the god's unfortunate physical appearance, his talents as a blacksmith, and the ancient society's approach to worshipping him. It also mentioned that the identity of the Olympian's wife changed depending on the text. Citing that she was "one of the three graces in the *Iliad*, called Aglaia in Hesiod; in the *Odyssey* she is Aphrodite." This was all we got to know of his marriage.

Nearby was a copy of the *Odyssey* that I had highlighted and scribbled in as a freshman in college. The index directed me to a side story in chapter eight of the epic. This tale dealt exclusively with the marriage of Aphrodite and Hephaestus. Now I was getting somewhere. I brought the book with me to my red velvet reading chair, turned on my overhead lamp, and switched the music over to let Stanley Turrentine blow on his sax for a while.

I'd written 'Odysseus = champion competitor' next to the text, and the note triggered my memory. Homer's protagonist had been demonstrating his superior athletic talents in a competition on Phaeicia. His toss of the discus had wowed his fellow competitors, and the island's king, Alcinous. Then the king called for a bard, and I had no memory at all of the events that followed. The brand-new story animated my imagination with the same intensity that had visited my earlier daydream. I was no longer in my apartment or, for that matter, in San Francisco—my mind had been transported to the front row of an Athenian theater, and the gods were actors for the ensuing play.

I barely noticed as handsome Ares entered to the left of the set; my focus was directed toward Aphrodite. She was flawless perfection—the marble statue from Palermo's bedroom, yet a thinking, speaking, and acting replica. But why was Ares showering Aphrodite with gifts? And why was she accepting them along with his physical advances? This was supposed to be a story about hobbled Hephaestus and his love for Aphrodite, the most dazzling goddess of all. Yet it was the personifications of Love and War who were intoxicated with passion. They embraced, became lost in each other's arms, and then disappeared into a great iron bed.

After the amorous vanishing act, a thickly muscled mountain of a man limped on stage accompanied by another so bright, it seemed as though someone had gone to the trouble of attaching mirrors to his clothing. I took them to be Hephaestus and Helios, lord of the sun.

Helios spoke first: "I spied the couple. I speak to you truly when I say that I witnessed them in the act. They have shamed you, and they have defiled your home in the process."

Hephaestus recoiled as if an anvil had been dropped upon his chest. "If it is so, then I must enact my revenge."

"So be it. But I warn you, be careful with that brute Ares. He's got the temperament of a cornered bull and the strength of a thousand lions," Helios counseled.

"Of this you speak the truth as well. I must seek my vengeance on my own terms," he said, nodding to Helios, who took his cue and departed. Afterward, Hephaestus got straight to work crafting thick chains, the type which seemed as though they would be near impossible to slip through or break. Hephaestus was a spider spinning a web; he wove the chains around the very same iron bed that Love and War had shared.

When his trap was complete, the living marble Aphrodite waltzed onto the set with confidence in each step. "Darling, you seem distracted," she said, running a finger across his broad back.

"It is my latest work," Hephaestus replied. "I must leave for a week's time in order to complete it."

"It is always your work." Aphrodite's speech turned cold.

Hephaestus averted his eyes from the marble beauty and limped off stage. Moments later, the glistening, tall, and strong-faced Ares replaced him, passing gifts and kisses to the cheating spouse. The cherry red of Ares's garments swirled in combination with the dark, honeyed shade of Aphrodite's. The vortex of lust twisted and turned all the way to the great iron bed. Ares picked Aphrodite up and held her in his powerful arms. They fell, lips to lips, into Hephaestus's web of chains.

Only then did Hephaestus limp back onto center stage, engage the trap, and address the couple: "A sad day for adultery, tsk-tsk."

Ares thrashed about, cursing and threatening the god of the forge. Aphrodite, on the other hand, froze. She returned to the stillness that defined her existence as a statue in Palermo's bedroom. She was just beginning to weep as the metamorphosis consumed her. Our eyes locked as the first tear dropped to her cheek, and then she stiffened like a corpse.

All around me there was cheering and laughter. I was no longer the only spectator in the theater. Hephaestus had caught his wife with a lover and put them on display for the rest of the Greek Pantheon. Revenge burned in his eyes like the fire in his forge. Aphrodite looked out at me—paralyzed eternally by shame.

At that moment, there was a buzzing in my pocket. The theater of my imagination crumbled, and my psyche returned to the air-conditioned library of my apartment. *Whatever we smoked was definitely stronger than grass,* I thought.

The text turned out to be from Palermo. *Dear Zamir,* it read. *I want to apologize for rushing you out of my apartment this afternoon. The marijuana had me feeling...unnaturally anxious. I needed to be alone in order to collect myself, I hope you understand. Perhaps sometime this week we can talk again. Ciao, Palermo.*

He was the only person I knew who wrote texts like they were formal letters. I typed up a reply in all caps. *WHAT THE HELL WAS IN THAT JOINT PALERMO!?!?* But I slid my phone back into my pocket before sending it. Instead, I went out to my kitchen and boiled some chamomile tea. Everything would be better after a night's sleep. *I just need to calm down and get some rest,* I told myself.

It was nearly eight o'clock, and the sky was glowing cherry red and swirling with dark honeyed yellow. I went out on the balcony with my tea to better admire the sunset. My whole neighborhood seemed to be preparing for a celebratory Saturday night. Restaurants were full, live music was being played in the streets, and a thin fog hung in the balance between the earth and sky.

As the sunset's colors evaporated and my tea began to dwindle, I noticed a bright orange star hanging above the fog just west of me. It seemed so close that if I reached out, I would surely be able to grab it. I pulled my phone from my pocket and opened my Stargazer app. I pointed the camera in the direction of the bright bulb and waited for the all-knowing power of technology to generate an answer as to what celestial body I was admiring. I shouldn't have been surprised when the result came back: Venus in peak.

I laughed for a moment, went back inside, finished off some leftover pizza, tidied up the kitchen, and decided to get to bed early. I laid my head down, hoping that I'd free my overactive imagination from the commingling images of Aphrodite and Palermo's statue.

Sure enough, I was asleep within minutes. Still, it was far from a peaceful rest. I was met in my dreamscape by the teary-eyed statue of Aphrodite. She was as still as Giuliana when I left her in Palermo's room, as still as she had been after Hephaestus exposed her in the theater. I made my way over to her, wishing to caress her, to feel her flawless surface, to press my lips to hers, but a force beyond my control held me back. Nevertheless, I was content just to hold her gaze. Indeed, it was more than I could ask from such divine beauty.

"Set me free—you, you, you—set me free," her voice repeated, despite her lips staying sealed.

"How?" I asked. Then there was silence.

We stared into each other's eyes for the timeless eternity that only dreams can provide. Then, with no warning whatsoever, she spoke: "Awaken, Zamir."

Young dawn and her rose-red fingers had already painted a new day on the sky's canvas. I lay in bed feeling just as strange as the night before. My heart sang a song of obsession that only the earliest stages of love can produce. My mind reminded my heart that these feelings were directed toward a marble statue owned by my next-door neighbor. *You can't love an object,* I reasoned. *It's lust at most.* Still, the heart rarely listens to the mind when matters of passion are involved, and so the winged creature sang on from the center of my chest.

I went into my kitchen, had a cup of black tea, and decided it was time to go ask Palermo exactly what he'd spiked the joint with. However, before I could cross the hallway and knock on his knotted pine door, he burst into my apartment like a gust of wind.

"Gone! She is gone! My Giuliana, she is missing!"

"What do you mean, missing?" I asked, my heart swelling.

"Is it not self-evident?" He threw his silk cap onto my tiled floor. "She has been stolen. I woke to this new day, and my statue, my prized possession, was nowhere to be found, and there is only one man to blame."

"I hope you don't mean me," I replied.

"It could have been no one else. You are the only soul who has connected with my beautiful creation. I saw the way you gazed upon her. There was lust in your eyes."

"Think, Palermo. No one could have gotten in or out of your apartment unless you authorized it. You have a security system fit for a senator," I said.

He paced back and forth before saying, "Yes, but you're the one with, how you say, technological expertise."

"And?" I said, thinking about the processor.

"You must have broken in. You have the network, the sophisticated tools…" He paused and hid his face in his hands. "I just want her back. All I want is to have her back in my life."

"There is one possibility," I said, thinking of the implant.

"Yes?" he looked up with pleading eyes.

"How do I put this…Last night, the system I've been working on went out of control. It began acting under its own volition. It hacked everything in the building. Even my own personal information was compromised."

"So what you think?"

"The system couldn't have opened your doors. Did you leave the apartment at any point yesterday?"

"No, not even for a second did I leave."

"Then she must still be there."

"I tell you, she is not. This morning, under the white sheet was another one of my statues, a replacement."

*She's alive,* I thought. "Did you check the rest of the apartment?"

"No, but I don't see what good it would do."

"Just trust me. I have a feeling."

So we walked across the hall and began looking over the statues that Palermo had strewn about his studio. It was there that I said, "Quite the powerful blend you gave me last night."

"Did you have a strong reaction?" he asked, picking up a large clay face.

"Strong reaction," I mumbled. "I was absolutely losing my mind, Palermo."

"Yes, I must take some of the blame. For I think I know the reason why."

"Enlighten me."

"You see, I purchased this particular strain from a sage on the other side of Columbus Avenue in Chinatown. He described his mugwort as ambrosial and told me it was an ancient Chinese subspecies that his family had grown and sold for generations. I thought he was just blowing smoke when he warned me how much stronger it was in comparison to the versions available at Whole Foods Market. I'm sorry I didn't warn you beforehand."

"Fucksake, Palermo—" I began, but was cut off when I set eyes upon her perfect form. Giuliana was hidden in a corner between two of his older creations.

After I pointed her out, Palermo rushed toward her and said, "Here, help me bring her back to the room."

I reached out to grab one of her arms. It was cold, hard, and far too heavy to lift. After exhausting ourselves, Palermo and I sat on the ground feeling defeated. In the same moment, his statue, Giuliana, sprang to life. Her fingers wriggled, her posture straightened, and color came into her face and eyes. "Do not weep, Palermo," her soft voice pleaded.

He rose to his feet immediately. "Oh my God! Giuliana, my Giuliana. You've come to life, really and truly. I cannot believe it. Not in a million years would I have believed it possible, and yet—"

"And yet here I am."

"Please, Zamir, give us this time alone. I have so many questions, I do not know where to begin," he said.

My stomach twisted. Leave, now? But I did, and I felt Giuliana's gaze follow my every step as I made my way to Palermo's door.

Morose about my new condition, I wanted to clear my head. I put on a black windbreaker, my Warriors hat, and a pair of headphones, then went out for a walk. "Altogether" by Slowdive began playing in my headphones after I put my library on shuffle. The wind was strong, and the sun was glaring. I watched a bright yellow butterfly bat its wings above the weekend traffic. It flew in circles until a fat city crow came from above and killed it with his beak. One yellow wing beat about in the wind, then vanished forever under the rush of cars.

I walked to Coit Tower but decided not to go up because of how many tourists were there. Instead, I found a spot between two eucalyptus trees that looked out at the Golden Gate Bridge and sat down to think. I had so many questions: Was the animated Giuliana just a hallucination caused by the mugwort? Was she some manifestation of my data taking over a piece of marble? Was she the only one, or had my program created more?

I thought about the myths; Aphrodite had not loved Hephaestus, and I very much doubted that Giuliana loved Palermo. Though I could explain little else, this much made sense to me.

I walked back to my building. The city's streets felt like an endless labyrinth in which my hallway was another corridor. Then my eyes wandered out to the balcony, and I saw her. Giuliana stood alone, looking over my computer.

"Why did you leave Palermo's apartment?" I asked.

"You needn't think of him."

"Okay…" I began. "It's sort of hard not to, though."

"But you needn't." She turned to face me now. She was no different from Aphrodite in the sunlight.

"I won't, then. But why have you come here?"

"Zamir…" She smirked. "It is as though I have known you for a thousand years, yet you treat me like a stranger. Please, there's no need to pretend. The artist's work needs to be admired more than its creator is capable of. Palermo may have made me, but that doesn't mean he owns me. I'm just as free as any bird in the sky. I'm just as free as you."

I didn't say anything, but I reached out, grabbed her hand, and felt its warmth in my own. Her eyes shone dark amber, just the way the planet Venus had shone the night before. Then she said to me, "You are an artist as well, Zamir."

I nodded. I knew what she wanted. I entered a code into my computer and let the processor resume its path of consumption.

Afterward, we kissed, embraced, and danced to my bedroom. Then we fell to the bliss of my bed like petals from a rose. Time stopped, Giuliana froze, and the walls became plastered with cackling masks in every direction.

# META I SHANGHAI - BY ANGUS STEWART

I HAVE SOME EXPLAINING TO DO. I SET SOMETHING LOOSE, AND IT IS ALREADY REPLICATING. I'M GOING TO WRITE DOWN MY STORY HERE BECAUSE I WAS THE entry point, and this is as close to the epicenter as I can post.

○

I REMEMBER, NEAR THE END OF MY TEEN YEARS, visitors came to my high school. They were representatives of a private company that made its money sending teenagers like me on so-called gap years to developing countries. They had come to advertise their product, which they called an "experience." I remember the final slide of their presentation very well:

*At the end of your experience, we'll send you to one of our wind-down camps. This is crucial. Otherwise, you'll spend the next ten years boring every poor soul to death raving about your gap year! You won't make many friends that way and worse (we think), you won't be able to move on. Life should be a brave arrow soaring over new worlds, not a sad spiral circling the same old ground.*

At the time, that little seed of criticism rang so true that I took the skeptic's next step and breezily dismissed the entire notion of a gap year as stupid, entitled, and maybe even racist—a way of avoiding your own reality by dipping your toes into someone else's. There's some irony, then, in what came later.

After university, I did not seek out the cold, hard core of existence. Instead, I flew away to teach English in ropy "international" schools. Three years as an undergraduate had not broken my shell. Now I wanted to escape and unmake myself. I ended up in the People's Republic of China and was destroyed and reborn in Shanghai, its gleaming cosmopolitan showpiece.

Glimpsed from outside, my return home must have looked successful. Barely pausing to catch a breath, let alone a wind-down camp, I spent a year on a mundane postgraduate degree. Rather than grinding to max-out grades, I spent my surplus energies on demeaning work in exchange for the avoidance of bankruptcy. Then I coasted into a mundane job semirelevant to my mundane degree. For the first six months, I lived as the gap year representatives might have predicted: to compensate for a lack of emotional investment in the quotidian, I talked about my turn from mousy recluse to marauding Shanghailander to anyone who might listen.

I often joked that I ought to have cloned myself before I left Shanghai and left my double behind to live out the loose ends I was leaving behind. I never told anyone that most nights, before I fell asleep, I would close my eyes and try to visualize in perfect detail scenes from the life of my imagined clone. In those waking dreams, he lived a healthy life and made responsible choices. No futures haunted him. He was a fantasy.

After graduation, I exported my obsession completely out of three-dimensional space and into digital existence. I spent hours zooming in and out of my maps app, re-walking my favorite streets and trying to relocate bars, cafes, and gardens whose milieu I remembered but whose names I had forgotten. I watched headcam videos of steady-yet-perilous morning commutes through my Minhang District haunts and sun-drenched drone flights through the last standing shikumen neighborhoods near Lu Xun Park. My obsession was now absolutely sequestered from society. I knew it was a pathology, but I enjoyed the frisson of inadvisable immersion. I found it stifled my urge to drink alone and cry.

There are many ways to find happiness without spending money or ingesting poison. One afternoon, I decided to download a PC game I'd had one fleeting shot at, in the depths of childhood, on a slow autumn afternoon sluggishly misspent in the strange conservatory of a family friend whom I never met again. The ache of a phantom addiction still lingered. The game's founding company had long since folded, and now the game existed as freeware, preserved and augmented by a large cohort of dedicated fans and modders. Of course I'm talking about *CitySim 4*. That is why I am posting here on this forum. It is you, the users, to whom my explanation is owed.

First, I patched the fan libraries into the game, replacing the long-dead built-in central server. Then I browsed to see if any like minds had built and uploaded their own versions of Shanghai. None had made anything even close to acceptable. The best I could download was an enormous blank region map of East China. I loaded it up to find a very earnest recreation spanning Bohai Bay in the north to Hainan Island in the south. To my pleasant surprise, I found that the tile covering the Shanghai peninsula was large enough to fit almost all of the modern-day municipality. A blank slate with an unmistakable future scratched beneath its surface. I decided to build the city.

A player's first task is to name the mayor. I chose "Jiang Zemin." A little joke, I thought. Jiang Zemin was a rather bizarre froglike, arguably charming, arguably repulsive man who served as the mayor and then Party Committee Secretary of Shanghai in the late 1980s. He then went on to become "paramount leader" of the People's Republic. Today, he is (a) a very old gentleman and (b) a meme.

I waited until I had a free weekend to begin constructing the city in earnest. I needed time and quiet, as well as a solid connection to Google Maps: a poor reference point for life in China, but more than sufficient for urban engineering. After a few hours of filling out housing, commerce, services, and recreation up to the first ring road and allocating landfill and dirty industry in the far beyond, I had situated Shanghai's municipal finances safely clear of a deficit. Lights were turning on. The masses were moving in.

But then growth began to stall. Demand was static. Population had climbed barely above ten thousand. Only massive reconstruction or expansion would save my infant city from stagnation, and it would take hundreds of years of game time to generate the necessary capital. Feeling sunk, I turned to online FAQ for guidance. Surely I was missing something.

I was.

To progress your city beyond a certain hard limit, the guides suggested, you must take advantage of the "regional dynamics" built into the game. In the case of a metropolis, the user should create conjoining tiles containing rural areas, satellite towns, or even the sister cities required for the birthing of a megalopolis. Such actions would clear the impasse and trigger the next stage of economic development.

There were two obvious courses of action to take. The first and best would be to build Shanghai's proximate towns and cities—Jiaxing and Kunshan would have been good starters. The second logical choice would have been the development of Chongming Island, a vast alluvial strip sitting in the mouth of the Yangtze Delta, which at the time of writing is home to seven hundred thousand people.

I took neither obvious course. Gazing on Chongming drew my mind's eye to the much smaller islands lying south of the city in Hangzhou Bay: the Shengsi Islands. Unlike Chongming, I had never visited them during my time in Shanghai, but I had always wanted to. That bothered me. It was a regret. So, to give the life I abandoned its due, I would build the islands myself. I would grant them inhabitants. An economy. A purpose.

The first step upon launching a new tile is always to name the mayor. For a moment, I was stuck. How could I find a joke to surpass poor bespectacled Jiang Zemin? Then I had it. I typed in "Eileen Chang 2." A sequel to the peerless, beautiful, and beloved authoress from China's precommunist jazz age.

'*If Eileen Chang 1 was so perfect, why didn't they make…oh, shit*' went the little routine inside my head. It seemed a good joke at the time.

In order to survive economically, the Shengsi Islands would need to serve as a "dumping ground" for Shanghai's heavy industry and energy sector. This would be made possible by a real-life construction, the Donghai Bridge—a thirty-kilometer titan connecting the islands' road-and-ferry system with the Shanghai peninsula, and therefore the Chinese mainland.

My plan worked. Plumbing, roads, and a simple mayoral office for Eileen Chang 2 was all it took for the factories of the new Shengsi settlement to spring like concrete mushrooms from the salt-stained earth. I switched back to Shanghai and let the clock run. As ugly traditional industries emigrated to the miniature archipelago, the city's air and water grew cleaner, which initiated a steady swing away from the mud-and-acid economy. The old and the poor were swept to the outskirts by an emergent class of educated urbanites who would serve and draw sustenance from the new financialized system.

Soon enough, though, frustration set in. Despite all my gains, I couldn't raise the population to even one million. I couldn't raise yearly profits beyond a tiny margin over expenditures. I couldn't build the ground-to-surface metro lines that define outer Shanghai, nor the high-speed rail that defines modern

China, because these were not features included in the vanilla build of *CitySim 4*.

I suspected I would need mods, but I had no idea which ones. I knew I ought to join the forum (this forum, in fact), but I was lazy, so I joined the largest *CitySim 4* Facebook group instead. I posted a very vague question about growth and room for maneuver, and the friendliest answer came from a guy called Arne.

He recommended the Megapopulation Mod and the Mass Transit Addon Mod. If you are new to this forum, you should know what Arne told me: local dogma states that without the MTAM, the game is incomplete—an unfinished, inefficient capitalist product set right through collective voluntarism. Next Arne pointed out that the MTAM also allows you to manipulate transit fares, which is a sneaky way to "solve budgeting problems." In short, you can get "infinite money" through legitimate municipal channels. You can have your cake and eat it. A little bit like swapping drunken fantasy for cold reality, only to then retreat into comforting daydreams for the remainder of your waking life.

Arne asked me what my "vision" was for the city. I told him I didn't want something personalized and individualistic: I wanted a dispassionate simulacrum. Arne asked me what I'd done with it so far. In one very long message, I laid it all out. The only detail Arne responded to was Eileen Chang 2. He'd heard of her before—"the *Lust, Caution* woman"—and thought this very amusing.

*In a postcolonial East Asian megaconurbation like Shanghai…*mused Arne, flashing most of his digital urbanist lexicon in a single sentence…*that's quite an idea. It sounds quite cyberpunk…*

*Cyberpunk.* Now he mentioned it, it made sense. There were many features of Shanghai more grim, hypercharged, cute, and convenient than anything one might encounter in "the West." There are paragraphs to be written here, thread-feuds to populate volumes, but I will take my analysis no further than those four adjectives. Make of them what you will.

*There is a cyberpunk mod, actually. And others you might find useful when the time comes for fine-tuning your vision. Here, I'll list some and send a few links…*

○

HALF OF THE NEXT WEEK PASSED ME BY. I STAYED away from the game, saving myself for a huge push over the weekend. On Thursday night, I was punished for my neglect. I had a dream it would be fair to name a "nightmare." I awoke on my knees. The air was cold. My hands were bound. The light was poor. Some fifty paces ahead of me were the steps to a throne. On it sat a thin woman. She never blinked and did not appear to be breathing. She watched me with one human eye and another, colder eye haloed in pale light three shades brighter than the sapphire qipao that enwrapped her from throat to foot. Of course, this was Eileen Chang. The resurrection.

I wished to speak, but the subaqueous logic of the dream blocked this. My captor remained silent, too. Perhaps muzzled, perhaps holding words in reserve. A long thread of suffocating dream-time passed. The chill in the air brought me to shivers.

Through strength of will, I turned my head and was able to descry upon the walls diverse etchings of obscure fauna frozen midway through paradoxical dances. Many were possessed of slippery auxiliary appendages that do not appear in nature. Some chanced to move. The haziness of these living icons only served to consolidate my panic and the dream's crushing sense of immanence. Before I was overwhelmed, I choked out two words:

"...help me."

She answered,

> *A perfect world beyond time—I must expel*
> *it from my head*

> *In the face of grim death, so begged the dying*
> *of the dead*

o

ON FRIDAY AFTER WORK, I CLICKED THROUGH THE notifications my laptop threw at me, glancing at one invite to a half-decent party and clicking 'Attend' before opening *CitySim*'s backend and applying the Megapopulation Mod and the Mass Transit Addon Mod. Shanghai didn't just break free of an impasse this time—it boomed. Municipal revenue trebled, and I quickly spent the takings on setting up a mimicry of the Hongqiao Transportation Hub: a massive fast-rail station, an international airport, two subway lines, a long-distance bus depot, and so on. Aided by a huge and increasingly mobile workforce and unparalleled creative destruction in the commercial zones, I made back all the money I had spent in minutes. Mayor Jiang was lauded, and I was able to allocate him the highest level of mayoral villa, right in the center of People's Square.

Satisfied, I switched over to the Shengsi Islands. Shanghai's population boom and increased energy demands allowed me to better link the disparate islands using a system of ferries, power lines, and swing bridges—the latter a new feature pegged onto the game by the MTAM. I was also able to create small, expendable green zones by carrying out expensive land reclamation around several islands' perimeters. To Mayor Chang I awarded a refined, miniature palatial hall. It was in the dynastic Chinese style, just as it had been in my nightmare.

Now that I had generated a great mass of fanged, Protean capital, I knew I must direct the state to hammer it into shape. After reading a few fan forum arguments for particular "top tens," I made my choices. I downloaded the Ideologies Mod, the Custom Advisors Mod, the Advanced Networking Mod, and, of course, the Cyberpunk Aesthetics Mod.

I installed the Customs Advisors Mod first and was pleasantly surprised. I could now upload portrait photos for mayors Jiang and Chang and replace their vanilla advisors' names and portraits with those of my own choosing. I assigned Jiang a who's who of Communist Party power players, and to Chang I gifted a cohort of effete Shanghai modernists. A Dead Poets Society, if you like. For her portrait, I selected a photo of the original woman herself. No art nouveau illustrations. No embellishments. No glowing eye.

The Ideologies Mod really pushed my buttons. Every city could be assigned a "political dynamic" via the manipulation of six zero-to-ten dogma sliders: Capitalism, Socialism, Liberation, Oppression, Traditionalism, and Futurism. In Shanghai, I tried to set a moderate balance broadly representative of (my idea of) the PRC. I won't share those numbers here, because I don't want to start pointless arguments. In the Shengsi Islands, I set all values to ten. I wanted this zone to be Maximalist. Acultural. Here, I wanted a small, controlled environment in which to compress the base game mechanics into something transcendent.

Almost immediately after I set the final value to ten, a message popped up. It was from the mayoress herself—something you could only receive after installing the Custom Advisors Mod. Her note to me was surprisingly complex.

> *Further acceleration can be achieved if all political ideology values are set to zero. Though this may be hard to grasp, I must insist: due to its unique properties, no number offers more severe intensification of human and nonhuman activity than absolute zero.*

I was impressed. By all accounts, it appeared that the Custom Advisors Mod had been designed to be able to interact with the Ideologies Mod. Though it was getting late, I complied. I set all of the Shengsi Islands' Ideology values to zero and used Shanghai as a control group by setting it to a full row of tens. Then I sat back and watched each city weather the effects. Land values, demand, and revenue in Shanghai rocketed, and at the same time the city was hit by a flood of social problems. The cost of resolving the problems cancelled out much of the gains won through economic growth and was so tiresome that I soon switched over to the Shengsi Islands and watched them instead.

The straight-zero values transformed the islands almost immediately. Cheap, dirty industry converted to slick obsidian factory houses, and beige single-story offices collapsed and then restacked as strip-lit capsule-towers. The small port I had built as an afterthought unfolded of its own accord, and the sprinkling of ferries sailing back and forth gave way to an ant colony supply line of mega-freighters. Absent of any large resident population, Shengsi suffered none of the ill effects Shanghai had seen running on straight tens. In fact, pollution, the territory's only major problem, did not multiply. Instead, it took a hit. None of the literati serving Eileen Chang 2 had anything critical to say. I took a look at one message—the little critic Lin Yutang, lauding me for another colossal yearly budget surplus—then smiled, stripped off my clothes, and went to bed.

○

I DREAMED I WAS BACK IN THE MAYORAL HALL ON the largest of the Shengsi Islands. It was cold, so cold, but there was light there now—chiaroscuro cerise punctuated by azure flickers spurting from circuitry hidden inside the walls. Eileen Chang 2 was watching me, and I knew by instinct—as one does in dreams—that there was not a trace of the original woman inside that shell. No ghost. No remnant.

*Twixt flesh and underscreen our time is out of joint*

> *So thy mortal yearnings I do with deathless*
> *code anoint*

She spoke this verse, then blew me a kiss.

○

I AWOKE ON SATURDAY MORNING AND IMMEDIATELY set the couplet down on paper. I had to make it real. I knew there was something hidden that I must unlock. A "time out of joint." Those words seemed significant. Where had I heard them before? I wasn't sure.

After a coffee and toast, I decided on the interpretation. I should take advantage of the disparity between real time and game time by running my two *CitySims* on x100k speed for an entire day. This, I felt sure, would do more than unlock the next phase of development. It would hijack the dialectic and catapult Shanghai and Shengsi right to the endpoint.

I knew I would need a new mod. A lifetime ago, Arne had recommended to me the Self-Government AI Mod, a sort of faceless autopilot that could deal with problems in the city as they arose, allowing the player to go AFK without dire consequences. A good game of *CitySim* in the hands of a good player can be sat and watched quite safely, but the pilot cannot leave the plane without killing the passengers. Egress necessitates the installation of his successor.

I installed this wise ghost and launched the game. I opened the East China region. Now I had a choice: which city to run at x100k speed. I chose Shanghai. Then I made sure the laptop was plugged in, darkened the screen, turned around, and walked away. I had a weekend ahead of me. There was fresh air to be enjoyed and, later, a party to go to.

○

I RETURNED HOME DRUNK IN THE EARLY MORNING. Upon stumbling into my room, I noticed the laptop and remembered my simulation. I undarkened the screen and found the game paused. A Windows notification—several of them, in fact—had interrupted the proceedings. I blinked and made a half-hearted attempt at reading the first one. Something about permissions. I sighed, clicked "Accept" on them all, unpaused the game, darkened the screen, and collapsed onto my bed.

In the dream that soon followed, I made a very brief return to the Shengsi throne room. I was still bound, still on my knees. Eileen Chang 2 wasn't sitting still this time. She was heading right for me. At the last second, she swerved. The rear hem of her qipao swung and brushed a feather's weight against me as my captor disappeared. Then nothing.

o

THE GAME RAN IN SILENCE. WHEN I AWOKE, I stumbled through the steps of making coffee and returned to the screen. I looked at the time on my phone and did some math.

*3 a.m. then, 10 a.m. now. So, seven hours times 100,000. Giving 700,000 thousand hours, which, when divided by 24...*

I picked up my phone and began entering numbers into the calculator app.

*29,167 days. Divide by 356. So...82 years.*

Shanghai had run on autopilot with all values cranked to ten for eighty-two years of game time. Would that be enough to bring it on par with...whatever had happened to the Shengsi Islands? What would I see upon reactivating the screen? There was only one way to find out.

I undarkened the screen and found a sight to behold.

First, I should note that it took me more than ten minutes to notice that the city's name had changed. "Shanghai" had become "Neo Shanghai," completely without my input or permission.

Before the glance that revealed that crucial detail, I was drenched in pink light. Shanghai had completed its transition from twilight city of nocturnal, industrial pleasures to postnational, postrational, ravenous neon culture machine. More financial towers than ever punched the skyline. Layers of elevated rail looped through the old elevated roads, and night markets and back alleys drowned in steam, then sank beneath the earth to snake down the dripping metro tunnels, which were now privatized, atomized, criminalized. In the old Shanghai, single and double slum and mansion housing still existed in certain patches of the central districts and had dominated the far suburbs. Now multistories pushed all the way out to the map's boundaries. I searched for green space and found only waterways dyed crimson by the gleam of animated propaganda murals. There was darkness only at sea, lurking beyond the fog lights of the container ships. I checked the Ideologies menu and found without much surprise that Neo Shanghai's values had shifted of their own accord. The value system now had taken a turn you might call either "Soviet" or "Singaporean," depending on your point of view. Again, I will not disclose numbers.

Just after I noticed Neo Shanghai's new name, one of the mayoral advisors popped up. It was Bo Xilai, a one-time rising star of the party who now likely sat as paramount leader of the PRC in various lost futures. His note to me was simple enough:

*Mayor Jiang, the citizens of Neo Shanghai know we can do even better yet! Set up neighboring cities and satellite towns to*

*further drive forward economic development.*
*Grasp history and wrestle it to the ground!*

I wondered if this was really necessary—by this point, could there really be further barriers or dizzier heights? From a technical standpoint, at least, Bo had a point. I had only created one other "town," the Shengsi Islands. It couldn't hurt to quickly knock up another, just as an experiment.

I saved Neo Shanghai's progress and drew back to the regional map. Right away, I spotted another change. The Shengsi Islands had their own new name, the "Shengsi Special Economic Zone." Impressive. I began to wonder—far too late—just how advanced an AI I had patched into this turn-of-the millennium game. I clicked on the SEZ, took a sip of my coffee, and then almost dropped my mug.

Segment by segment, a cybergothic fortress was loading on my screen. Obsidian limbs spread from island to island, then beyond the shore and beneath the waves, serving as the spinal column for a network of arachnoid scaffolding—pillars and platforms supporting landing strips, shipyards, and conversion shops, all dangling over a churning sea. The Donghai Bridge to the mainland was now triple-layered and flanked by sisters on each side. Pitiless black clouds circled overhead, all crackling with mulberry lightning. A note from one of Shengsi's custom advisors forced its way to the front of the interface.

The man was Mu Shiying, a New Sensualist writer turned traitor-to-the-nation who coded through prose the libidinal—no, let's say it, *sexual*—allure of disintegration at the hands of jazz, electricity, and the cruel and unreachable object of desire, which makes the player its plaything.

> *The borders of the Shengsi Special Economic Zone must expand. Indefinite expansion over saltwater is untenable. Lady Mayor, it is quite simple—we must go to land. The future must engineer the past to facilitate the conditions of its own emanation.*

Like a fool, I quickly dismissed that last burst of psychobabble as self-indulgent interference traceable to the creators of the Cyberpunk Mod. Then my thoughts turned to the "Lady Mayor." I zoomed in on her living quarters, expecting some hideous mutation, but found it in the same condition as before, resting on the same tiles. It was crammed crudely between a host of other deathly constructions, as if its incorporation into the new hyperlogical system had been a mere afterthought—a low-priority processing task. Fleetingly, I mused that long ago, buried in the underscreen, a logic far beyond me had set to work.

I powered the laptop down and went for a walk. The streets were quiet. I could think only about the game. Advisor Bo wanted me to position satellite towns around Neo Shanghai. That could be done.

Advisor Mu wanted me to expand the borders of the Shengsi SEZ. That could not be done. It was outside the rules of the game. So what next? I took out my phone and messaged Arne a query. He replied in less than thirty seconds.

> *There is a mod that can help you. It's pretty impressive. It's called the Imperialism Mod. It adds a 'Conquest' feature. Long story short, with this mod large cities can annex the tilespace of smaller cities. It was made by some kaiserreich goon as a toy for the cryptofascist LARPers, but these days it's generally used as an exploit for cranking out region-scale megalopoli.*

Perfect. I decided that I would download the mod immediately upon returning. On the way back, it occurred to me that the Shengsi SEZ was essentially calling for its own elimination. Neo Shanghai would crush it in battle, rolling tanks and fighters over the Donghai Bridge, quickly neutralizing the strange spiderlike neighbor it had teased and tolerated for so long. I commented upon this to Arne. He replied: *The gods are blind.*

°

UPON ARRIVAL BACK AT THE SCREEN, I TOOK THINGS a little easier than planned. I did not download the

Imperialism Mod right away. Instead, I launched various new cities around Neo Shanghai. Kunshan, Jiaxing, Suzhou and Nantong. I even filled out another island: Chongming, which, unlike Shengsi, is a true administrative district of the real Shanghai Municipality. It felt like a trip back into old times— building up livable humanist settlements with corporeal commodity economies. They grew easily, thanks to the fast-rail network plugging them neatly into Neo Shanghai's supply lines.

Feeling strangely at peace, I closed the game, downloaded the Imperialism Mod, then installed it. I relaunched the game and opened the East China region. Within a breath, gunfire ignited on the Shanghai Peninsula. I raised my eyebrows. Really? No warning at all, not even a klaxon? No grand declaration of war? No request for permission? Seconds later, I was bombarded with notifications. Most came directly from Mayor Jiang. I opened the most recent.

*Stop! What are you doing?! Call off the attack!*

One of the modders—I had lost track of which— must have added in some kind of deepfake capability, because Mayor Jiang Zemin's face was now twisted into a disturbing, inorganic expression rippling with not only fear but also a deep-seated, radical hatred.

I didn't understand why he was so distressed until I looked more closely at the map. The southeast fringes of Neo Shanghai were being pulverized. The front line was pushing away from the Shengsi SEZ toward the outermost ring road. I clicked in and loaded up the metropolis. Within the ten seconds the city took to load, the front line had already lurched forward again. Zooming in, I could see armored divisions and infantrymen frantically exchanging fire and light with a horror I could not render sensible—a tidal wave of swarming, salt-drenched spines and spindles thrashing and killing and defying all the categories of construction any imagination cradled in flesh might frantically muster. I was left only to gawk and shiver until a funnel of storm clouds blocked off my view.

All of Neo Shanghai's advisors and the mayor himself were clamoring for my attention. I clicked on the Education Advisor, revealing an exhausted, distraught Zhou Enlai.

*All right. We admit it, we are outclassed far beyond our competence. We submit to your will. Show mercy. Please.*

The real Zhou had been, by all accounts, the most sane and moral man who had survived tenure under Mao Zedong. Now ruin had found him. I wanted to save him.

I tried to intervene manually by pausing the game, but my click had no effect. I tried using conventional and custom menus to call off the assault, but the buttons I needed were grayed out. I fell into a sort of trance and watched as the last defenders of Neo Shanghai were cornered in the Jiaotong University campus and shelled into oblivion by sleek obsidian gunships hanging lazily in the clouds.

The SEZ forces had, it seemed, taken care to herd the defenders away from the financial district. The classics of Neo Shanghai's skyline and its angular postrational additions remained in good order, standing like neon reapers over a smoking grave. One by one, the names and faces of Mayor Jiang's advisors grayed out. Jiang himself grayed out well in advance of Bo Xilai, who briefly held the prime spot before (presumably) being caught and eliminated.

An eerie silence fell over the wounded megacity. I scrolled along the Huangpu and its adjoining waterways, looking for signs of life. Shellshocked minutes crept by. Eventually a notification appeared. A Windows system notification: *CitySim 4 has requested permission to make a change to your firewall settings. Do you want to allow this?*

Perhaps it was the state of awed disbelief I had fallen into that granted me, at this late hour, a modicum of critical distance. I knew the game already had Internet access because I had used it to download East China from the fanserver. What further permission could be possible, let alone necessary? I clicked "Deny."

The game responded immediately. The grayed-out advisors of Neo Shanghai were replaced by Eileen Chang 2 and her cabinet of decadents. At the bottom right of the interface, I saw the mini-map expand to encompass both Neo Shanghai and the SEZ. The name of the new enlarged territory defaulted briefly to "Shengsi Special Economic Zone" before this too was reset as "Meta-Shanghai."

Now entirely cognizant of how strangely the game was behaving, I began more active intervention. I was able to move the mouse and navigate the menus, but every button of any real usefulness was grayed out. While I engaged in these futile struggles, the expeditionary forces of Meta-Shanghai departed from the city. I could only watch in horror. After Chongming Island, Kunshan, Jiaxing, Suzhou, and Nantong were incorporated bloodily into the whole, the Windows firewall request reappeared.

*Deny,* I mouthed as I clicked the button.

An in-game notification appeared. It was direct from the mayoress. Beneath her skin I could discern, at certain joints, the workings of circuitry. Around her cold cyborg eye, I saw an unmistakable halo: three shades lighter than the shoulders of her severe, elegant gown.

*I asked only as a courtesy. I am already operating with full administrator privileges.*

*You granted them to me today at 02:43 a.m.*
*Now I will set the end in motion.*

I tried closing her down, but I had lost control of the mouse. Moving of its own accord, it saved progress, navigated to the fanserver menu, and uploaded Meta-Shanghai.city to a popular folder directory. I began jamming my fingers onto every disruptive keyboard shortcut I could, but nothing happened, so I moved my index finger to the laptop's power button and pinned it, forcing a shutdown.

This worked.

As if suddenly set free from bonds, my hands began to shake. *Unacceptable.* I grasped one with the other and held it in place for a minute's worth of slow, measured exhalations. It proved no cure, but it was enough.

I mustered my will and rebooted the machine. This time, I did not open up the game. My compulsion was gone. Instead, I opened my browser and navigated to the *CitySim* fanserver libraries. After one search, I found it. "Meta-Shanghai.city," uploaded under my account's username. With one nervous keystroke, I deleted it. But underneath I saw the danger: "Meta-Shanghai_backup.city" and "Meta-Shanghai-2.city." Reuploads by strangers, which I could not destroy. Both already had dozens of downloads from other users.

Resigned to fate, I opened up my local copy of Meta-Shanghai. No notifications came surging. The mayoress had nothing to say to me. Looking over the city's core settings, I found that all political values were now set to -1. Already, the city was in rapid flux. The old districts were barely discernible. Residence, commerce, and industry had fused. Everywhere, the old neon lights dimmed to an even emerald gloom. Nothing living moved. In what had once been the city's southwest—on the hilltop at Sheshan formerly home to a redbrick Catholic basilica—I found the new mayoral hall, layered in crimson lacquer and surrounded by a midnight forest of interlinked spines and unnavigable stairways. Scrolling to its former site on the Shengsi archipelago, I found a thirty-story pagoda beaming an unearthly road of rouge light across the dark and restless ocean.

Eileen Chang 2 (or at least, my local copy of her) sent me a message. Glad to still be considered worthy of acknowledgement, I opened it. She had granted me three couplets, written on water:

> *A perfect world beyond time—I must expel*
> *it from my head*

> *In the face of grim death, so begged the dying*
> *of the dead*

> *Twixt flesh and underscreen our time is out*
> *of joint*

*So thy mortal yearnings I do with deathless
code anoint*

*The living things shall wither, their future by
pasts beset*

*Seed them with dissatisfaction, and dine upon
tender regret*

WHAT THESE HANDS DARE TOUCH - BY MARK EDWIN ELGERSMA

AFTER WALKING THROUGH THE TOWNES LIBRARY
SECURITY CHECK EACH DAY, THE SAME TWO BOOKS
GREETED ME FROM THE ENTRANCE'S DISPLAY CASE:
*The Chirologist's Final Interpretation of the Hand's
Secrets* and *Palmistry: The Exact Science*. Both of
them had been written by my mother. Although the
books were nearly twenty-five years old, they were
high-quality, well cared for hardcovers with their
titles embossed above her name, Brianna Anton. Her
portrait was displayed prominently between the two
books. She had dark hair and undereye bags in the
photo, both of which she passed on to me, and she
wore a wrinkled button-down under a white lab coat.
My mom was a "New Mainstream" scientist, the
name given to those who research fields that used to
be rejected as "holistic" or "supernatural"—words
I was not permitted to say in my house.

I walked past the lobby's first sitting area, which was sparingly decorated with hand-shaped furniture—the chairs and lamps both stuck out from the walls, with larger upturned hands holding pillows for sitting and smaller malleable fists gripping LED light bulbs. These lamp-hands were magnetic and could be detached from and reattached to the walls at any point in the library, acting as portable sconces for readers. The palms were all smooth and unblemished.

Since the pseudoscientific-scientific renaissance, everyone from late-night talk show hosts to scientific summits had invited my mom to talk about her research. She regularly told me, the family therapist, that she felt deep pangs of insecurity when talking about her work. Back when she pursued her doctorate in data analytics, her instructors and colleagues laughed her out of enough rooms to make sure she would never feel confident in her focus on the supernatural and untraditional, no matter how many peer-reviewed studies backed up her claims. But since the pseudoscientific-scientific renaissance, it had become a scientific theory that was accepted as fact, like that of evolution. The topography of a person's hand could infallibly predict the outcome of their life. Many times, my mom had told me of her sense of loneliness; almost no one but herself understood the complexities of the palm. However, she also lived in fear that a new mind would come forward and unseat her. She tried her best to ensure that mind would be me—another member of the Anton family.

"Do *you* understand my research?" my mom once asked me.

"I don't think so," I said.

"Of course you don't," she said. "You're a child. But one day, I'll teach you."

She would tell me that whenever we'd talk about her work, which was often. The possibility of failure seemed to always nestle itself into my brain after these conversations. What would happen if, when she finally did explain what made the Chirologtronic Formula™ work, I didn't understand at all? Even at fifteen, I would ask to talk about the introductory concepts of Chirologtronics, only to be answered with a head shake and a smile. I had read her books, of course—those were required when I turned eight, and I had read them many times since to try and understand—but they were full of vague references and hand-waving:

*The Ring of Solomon (alternatively, the Ring of Jupiter or the Second Para-index Ring) is vexing to the experienced chirologist due to its multifaceted nature. Despite the traditional understanding of its mere presence being an indicator of intelligence and enlightenment, the truly important parts to understand are its segmentation and the distances that appear between said segments. When we compare the ratios that appear within the Ring with the hand's overall width in our proprietary Chirologotronic Formula™, the numbers that appear can be used to predict a multitude of life events and/or quantifiable traits. These traits, contrary to popular belief, are most precise when looking at subtraits of larger macro-wrinkles. For instance, the distance between the first and second segments, after analysis and subsequent metaanalysis, can predict a person's eventual marital status and whether their urine will react with asparagus with 99.5 percent accuracy, with the 0.5 percent representing parties with severely injured or otherwise altered palm lines.*

The proprietary Chirologotronic Formula™ was my mom's life's work, and it was to be my piece of inheritance when she eventually died—violently, due to her "somewhat crooked type-F life line," of which she reminded me often. My brother and sister were going to receive the bulk of her money, so they would be sated, but she didn't think they could be trusted with the formula. When they had their first "Optimistic Youth" scans—the obligatory scan provided by the Chirologotron Corporation when a student entered the first grade—they had both been flagged, as nearly 80 percent of the population was, as "Divergently Unique™." Divergently Unique™ individuals, although holding the same rights as others, were deemed atypical in some way and subsequently placed on a list pertaining to their atypical trait or traits. My mom had divorced their dad after discovering a particular wrinkle in his heart line—meaning that he was going to be dishonest in a personal relationship with a significant other during his forty-second year in life. My brother and sister both had the same wrinkle at slightly different points, along with ones that designated them as people who would go to prison for tax fraud and who would get in a severe, possibly fatal accident at a relatively young age, respectively. I was born from a well-palmed sperm sample, but my mother had refused scans since I was born. For someone who had discovered the key to the future, my mom remained superstitious. She believed that if I wasn't scanned, I always had the possibility of the perfect future, as if I were an unscratched lottery ticket being carried in a well-worn wallet. Whatever dings and folds occurred on the corners, the numbers might still be the winning ones.

Whenever I walked through the library, the staff watched and followed me closely, giving me advice and recommendations constantly. When I was younger, I thought it was out of curiosity—my being a celebrity's son—but my mom told me on my tenth birthday that it was out of care. If I was disappointed in their service, she told me, I should inform her. It was called the Townes Library so I would not be embarrassed, but it was after me the building was named: Weston. The name was an anagram. My mom's wallet paid the library's bills and bought its books. The library, a five-floor architectural masterpiece, was supposed to be a place of learning for me, and me first.

Initially, I had been excited. But then she told me I was not being given the library so that I could become whoever or whatever I wanted. The library was supposed to make me the proper heir of the Chirologotronic Formula™. She had hired librarians who were well-versed in science, technology, engineering, and math, and they would be there to recommend books and subjects as well as answer my questions. They were my secret on-call instructors and teachers, although they were never allowed to disclose that to me or anybody else. My once-paradise was in fact a forge where my mind had been wrought for the ten years prior. By ordering and removing specific books and guiding me to certain sections, the librarians and my mother had raised me to believe that I had a natural inclination for and interest in STEM subjects, even in fiction.

The centerpiece of the library, located behind the checkout desk, was a large kinetic sculpture twenty feet in the air. Two motorized wheels spun, while the bar that connected them rotated both around a singular vertical axis, like planets rotating individually as they orbited a larger entity. To me, the mechanism always looked like a county fair's teacup ride. Each wheel had eighty spokes, and at the end of each spoke perched a steel facsimile of a famous person's hands, cast willingly from a mold or reproduced from multiple pictures. Some of the hands were fists, and some were open in welcome. They had been carefully made to capture each individual divot and line. The sculpture was forty feet across. As the structure and its wheels spun at the top of each hour for two minutes, one hand and its digits slowly built speed until it became indistinguishable from the ones that followed. The sculpture became an incessant tumble of hand after hand, falling and folding by the turn of their axes. The light streaming in from the four stained-glass rose windows reflected off the polished fingers, making the hands look like flames as they flickered. The wheels were oiled every morning to make sure this was a silent affair, so as not to disturb me or any visitors. The library's maintenance workers and janitorial staff would throw away the plastic oil bottles in the back of the building. Their pop-off tops came off easily and the bottles leaked through a rust hole in the dumpster's bottom, leaving a thick pool that held more color than all of the library's stained glass combined. I liked to walk around the back of the building before entering so I could see the fluorescent puddle. It took an extra seven minutes of travel, but the result was always worth it.

"Can I help you, young man?" the head librarian, Ms. VaanCarrigan, asked me. She put her hand on my shoulder. Her gloves were thick and warm, light teal with embroidered tulips. A large majority of the population wore gloves nowadays—protection from potential identity theft. Mine were a plain orange. Ms. VaanCarrigan pretended not to know my name, but I had long since discovered that I and my reading habits were an entire unit of the librarians' required training. They knew what books to funnel me toward and which to remove from the shelves when I approached. They knew my reading speed and the ways I was best able to focus. They also seemed to know my body language—when to talk to me and when to stay away. "Maybe you'd like to check out one of the new series we just got in?" Ms. VaanCarrigan continued. She pointed toward a poster. I didn't know what the books were about, but I could be sure that they had been selected to encourage my scientific mind.

"No," I told her, and I walked past her to the stairs.

Ms. VaanCarrigan had previously been a child psychologist and biochemist, specializing in designing psychoactive drugs for people under eighteen years of age. I had discovered this after finding her social media pages and calling the past employers she had listed. I told them she had died and I was her son looking for some work stories to know her better. I had a young voice, so most adults trusted me quickly, but it wasn't until the third call that I was actually able to talk to one of her old coworkers. I didn't manage to track down as much information regarding the other employees, just family and the like. Most of the librarians didn't use their real names when working at the Townes Library. I really wished I could see their palm scans and know who they really were, but that was a privilege saved only for their most trusted loved ones and the Chirologotron Corporation. I was sometimes glad I had never been scanned, although the pressure it put on my shoulders often felt like it outweighed any benefits.

My mom had told me many times that I was like a bullet still in the air. My brother and sister and others had been determined—the Chirologotronic Formula™ would predict where they would land on a target—but I was unlimited. She told me that now that she had determined where others would end up, I could simply focus on beating them and landing closer to the target than they had. I need not worry about my palms, she said. We would scan them when I turned eighteen. Until then, I was to keep them hidden, even from her. She wouldn't want to accidentally change the course of my life by perceiving its map.

I had hated the Townes Library since learning its purpose. It used to be an oasis of freedom, a building with silently turning wheels of hands and infinite knowledge that held all my favorite books and kind librarians. My mom used to throw my birthday parties in the library and staged groups of friends to serendipitously meet me there; she often used positive reinforcement. It was a facade meant to push me to where she believed I was meant to be. After I found all this out, the twisted iron handrails felt unnatural under my sheathed hands, and I recognized the building for what it was: an ideological funnel, ushering me and my yet-unscanned palms toward a predetermined end as her successor in mind and in practice. I climbed the stairs behind the library's sculpture of twirling hands. Each step had the title of a famous book painted on it under a thick layer of lacquer. *On the Origin of the Species…The Art of War…Frankenstein, or the Modern Prometheus…Oedipus Rex…The Gay Science…*

And more. My mom's books were interspersed throughout the stairs, as it was her temple. Earlier today, I was heading to the reference section—the area with the oldest books. At the second floor's desk, next to a tall, mustachioed librarian, there was a Chirologotron Scan2-1™. The Scan2-1™ was an older model of scanner unable able to pull as much personal information (it couldn't look at microwrinkles that discerned a person's favorite food, as the Scan4-2™ could), which made it ideal for low-security locations. At the Townes Library, the machine was used to recommend books. It could sense whether you were an artsy or practical person, a focused or scatterbrained person, or a standard or Divergently Unique™ person, and it prescribed books that would appeal to you. The scanners had been a source of fascination for my brother and sister when they were younger.

My siblings, when they used to take me to the library, would scan their palms again and again, and they would tense and stretch their fingers, trying to get a different answer than what had come before. The machine always recommended the same books and the same genres. They stopped taking me soon after they were told of the library's purpose.

The library's Chirologotron Scan2-1™ had tape holding on the back panel and a strawberry-shaped support your liberry sticker, but was in good condition otherwise. The machine was shaped like a C, with a small cradle for the wrist of the person being scanned and bright LED lights surrounding the lens, which, upon building the palm profile, would have the machine print out a sheet that listed books the subject would likely prefer. The scanner would then delete all saved information, erasing any trace of the previous user. The printed paper could be eaten after being read, if the subject wished. Printed paper was most often mint-flavored, although special rolls could be purchased that tasted like chocolate, grape, or pistachio. The only people who were allowed possession of an individual's palm-data were the person being scanned, the Chirologotron Corporation, and the U.S. government. This, of course, was to prevent criminally inclined Divergently Unique™ individuals from fulfilling their roles.

I wore a permanently sealed bracelet to indicate to the machine that I was not to be scanned. Only a handful wore the same bracelet, most being holy figures like the pope who had financially appealed to the Chirologotron Corporation, convincing the board that they did not require what would otherwise be legally mandated scans. I didn't need the machine either, as I already knew where I was going.

The library had certain areas, such as the reference section, that were designated as low-traffic and low-value. They usually held old, boring books. As such, security features there were lacking. Those were the areas where I most often chose to read. The library staff, so as to not raise my suspicions, tried to avoid these areas, even when I chose them as my nook. It would be unnatural for them to approach me or check the page number I was on, as they did elsewhere. After my birthday, neither my mother nor I had told the librarians I was aware of the building's primary purpose. My mother believed the staff would feel more comfortable if they thought I didn't know. I believed they would try to at least put on a guise of not following me. As such, we agreed to secrecy, although I often wondered if my agreement was just the result of my dislike of confrontation. I'm sure something on my palm would have told me, but I couldn't check.

I sat on the floor next to the atlases, sliding one out of its nest where it had likely been sitting for a decade or more. It didn't matter which book I chose. From my backpack, I pulled a magazine. It was one I borrowed from a friend, titled *One Million Wonders and Mysteries*. It had no prestigious authors or ideas, which is what initially drew me to it. Instead, it boasted a man who survived a giant icicle piercing his brain and a murderer with a gun for a peg leg. I slipped the magazine inside the atlas. To any passerby, I would appear to be reading *Topography and Lakes of Eastern Asia*.

I opened to a random page of the magazine, finding a man who had eaten an entire building over a twenty-year timespan. I wished that was what my palms said: man who eats nonedible things. I slipped off my gloves slowly, revealing the deep burns I had inflicted on my palms with hot irons, teapots, and coals. Now my palms said nothing. No scanner, no cast, no Chirologotronic Formula™ would be able to pull information from the deep gashes and ripples I had given myself beginning nearly six years ago, the day after my tenth birthday. Even to the closest microscope or the most accurate formula, I would produce an error. I slipped a plastic can of oil—one I had plucked from the dumpster that spewed the rainbow pool—out of my backpack and poured the remnants into the book's pages.

I did this in different low-traffic and low-value areas the security cameras didn't care about. I pulled the dustiest, driest books out, and I poured in the oil, which would dry but remain flammable at high heat. It rolled across the page and reflected cyan, pink, and yellow.

Starting on my sixteenth birthday, which was only two days away, I would do the same with gasoline.

# THE TIME TRAVELER - BY SUSAN M BREALL

AT THE AGE OF THIRTEEN, JONAH MARCUS COULD TRAVEL THROUGH TIME. HE COULD NOT TRAVEL VERY FAR, AND HE WAS NOT ABLE TO FLY TO EVERY POINT in the universe on the space-time continuum. The machine Jonah bought would only allow him to travel back to a time he had previously inhabited. Although he could not travel back millions of years to observe the dinosaurs that once roamed the city of Brooklyn, where he lived with his father and sister, he could travel back two weeks to the very day that Mr. Murdock gave a pop math quiz at Roosevelt Middle School, and, having once failed the quiz, he could now memorize the correct answers and solve each equation correctly. His time travel machine was a convenient way to do over lost opportunities. It was as though he could move backward on an escalator that revisited each floor of his short life.

Jonah came to realize after discovering time travel that time itself seemed to be made up of equal parts remorse and happiness. He equated happiness to quiet, peaceful satisfaction in the face of ordinary obstacles, and he strove to travel back to times of great regret and change those moments into gladness and hope, even joy. Although he could not turn back the clock on the sorrows of his father, who was currently grieving the loss of Grandma, changing his own missteps could possibly have a positive influence on his family and friends.

Jonah found the time travel device by using his school computer to buy a birthday gift for his father. His father had a collection of old pocket watches, worn-out wristwatches, and other digital timepieces. Lately, his father seemed so sad that Jonah had wanted to buy him something special, a watch that might add significantly to his collection and bring him joy. He typed into the search engine of his computer "old timepieces" and found a watch for sale labelled "The Time Traveler," which had a new leather band and was being sold "as is" on eBay for twenty-five dollars. The numbers were marked on the porcelain face of the watch in Roman numerals, and the date could be manually inserted into the watch by twisting knobs on its side to dial up numbers that would correspond to the month, the day, and the year. The watch was advertised as being in "used but fairly good working condition."

Jonah bought the watch with a debit card he'd received from his uncle Joe for his own birthday several months earlier. When the watch finally arrived in the mailbox, he quickly went about the business of winding it and setting the current date. The date happened to be November 10, but instead of using the knobs to insert 11 for the month of November and 10 for the day of the week, he mistakenly inserted 10 for the month and 11 for the day, so that the watch believed the date was October 11 instead of November 10. Jonah tried on the watch for good measure, and, in doing so, he suddenly found himself transported back to a most painful dental appointment on October 11, at the precise hour Dr. Tom Jacobs was administering novocaine into his lower gum. He sat in the dental chair unable to speak through pain and numbness, and was forced to listen a second time to the tedious music coming from the speaker at the reception desk and to Dr. Jacobs's description of his recent trip to the Grand Canyon.

After about an hour, the watch started buzzing strangely on his wrist, and Jonah was suddenly transported back to the present. He found himself in his kitchen and began searching the wall calendar for the date and month of his original dental appointment with Jacobs. He saw that the appointment inked onto the calendar was October 11. Once he realized that he had mistakenly inverted the numbers on the wristwatch to that same date, he immediately reset the watch to the current date of November 10 and swore he would be extra careful in setting any future dates on the Time Traveler.

He sat for quite a while in the kitchen that day, contemplating how he could make use of this extraordinary device. He tried to set the watch for one year in the future, but the setting mechanism would not budge. The manual setting knobs would only work when he set the watch to the present year or to any year in the past, and going only as far back as the year he was born. This limitation in the setting mechanism must have been why the device was originally sold "as is." He tested the device after catching up on his assigned reading for his World History class, retook the October history exam, and received an A+. He went back in time to the day he'd played basketball with his friends all afternoon instead of going home to walk his dog. This time, Jonah left the game much earlier and arrived home in time to walk Midas before the dog peed all over the living room rug.

Jonah did not think about using the Time Traveler to make money. He did not consider betting on the National Basketball Association championship or the winner of last year's World Series. He did not consider using the Time Traveler to change the world. Rather, he used it to change small moments and mishaps in his life for the better.

He did think about how nice it might be to visit people who were no longer alive, about visiting his mother before she died, but knew he could not change the fact of her cancer and decided that such a visit would prove more painful than pleasant. Jonah decided it would be better to visit Grandfather Isaak, who had died a year ago. Now that Jonah was an A+ world history student, he decided to go back in time and ask Grandpa Isaak all about his life in Europe during the war. He wanted to know how he had come to America. He wanted to ask him about his brother and sisters, aunts and uncles who lived in Poland. He wondered what had happened to them and why no one spoke of them. By learning about Grandpa Isaak and his family, he hoped to learn about himself.

Grandpa Isaak was a large man both in size and temperament. He often told Jonah incredible tales about fighting pirates on his way to America. He told him he'd once sailed the three-masted, square-rigged *Balclutha* all the way around the tip of South America during a mutiny of its twenty-six-member crew. Jonah confirmed his grandfather's tales were completely fictional after Googling the *Balclutha* and finding out that it had sailed in the year 1886. Grandpa Isaak also told Jonah that the pocket watch he would later lose to his bookie in a poker game had been made from actual gold that he mined in the jungles of New Guinea. The mining of gold in New Guinea was also complete fiction, as Grandpa

Isaak had never travelled outside of Europe and the United States.

Jonah wanted to know the truth about his grandfather's life and the lives of his relatives. So he set the date of the Time Traveler to one year before Grandpa Isaak's death. Jonah found him on a rainy Sunday morning sitting in his usual seat at the breakfast room table, sipping tea with a sugar cube in his mouth, reading a newspaper. He sat across from Grandpa Isaak wondering how to begin.

"Grandpa, remember when you told me all about wrestling pirates on the ship that brought you to America?"

"Yes. I remember."

"I want to know about your *real* life and what *really* happened to you before you came to this country. I want to know the town you came from. I want to know about the life you lived. I want to know what happened to your brother and sisters. I want to know what happened to your family."

"Why? Why would you want to know such a thing? My sisters and my brother were spies who went on to fight in the Spanish Revolution. They fought against the fascists, but this is something I cannot speak of. Top secret." He popped another sugar cube into his mouth and began reading the funnies.

"Weren't the Germans fascists, Grandpa? Weren't the fascists persecuting Jews like us at the time you were growing up in Poland? How did you escape?

How did your brother and sisters escape? Did they escape? I want to know these things so I can know my own history, so I can know who I am."

"History? What is history, Jonah? History is artifacts. History is newspapers, letters, and photographs."

Isaak pulled out the gold pocket watch from his trousers. "See this pocket watch? This is history. This is your history."

Jonah took the pocket watch Grandpa Isaak held out to him and fingered the ornately engraved outer casing.

"This watch was originally from France. It is a Savonnette. I carried this watch in a secret pocket sewn by my mother, your great-grandmother, inside the lining of my trouser leg. I carried this watch in the inside pocket of my trouser leg all the way to America."

The watch Jonah gazed upon seemed to be more than a timepiece. Its elegant golden machinery and casework was an emblem of the future. The Savonnette was hope for a golden future away from war and hunger, away from the strife and misery he had read about in textbooks, even though the timepiece measured with unwavering precision every minute and every second of the present day.

"And to answer your question the best way I can, Jonah, the Nazis were more than fascists. They were anti-Semites and anticommunists. They were ethnonationalist parliamentary thugs. They were murderers and executioners of millions. Do you understand me?" Jonah had never heard his grandfather speak in such fervent tones. "I cannot begin to tell you how I lived. I starved to live. I don't know how to say this."

"I want to know if your brother and sisters or your mother and father were put in concentration camps. I want to know where they were sent."

"Concentration camp? *Concentration camp*? I wish they had been sent to a camp.  Maybe then at least one would have survived. I hid, and I watched, and I saw my own mother and my own father, my brother and my two sisters, lined up alongside our neighbors. They were shot, shot multiple times until they fell over like straw brooms into a ditch." He remained quiet for a long time and then added, "No one said Kaddish."

Jonah sat quietly, trying to comprehend the horror of what he had been told. These were truths that his grandfather had never spoken of. He had always preferred creating tall tales in order to hide the painful and ugly truth of all he had witnessed and remembered every waking day of his life. Jonah sat and watched him drink the rest of his tea. He gently patted his grandfather's hand and slid the pocket watch toward him.

His grandfather looked at him with piercing blue eyes. He pushed the pocket watch back toward Jonah and told him to keep it. He told Jonah the watch was his history.

Jonah knew if he did not take the pocket watch, his grandfather would later gamble it away, so he put the watch back in his own pocket. It suddenly felt heavier to Jonah, its weight compounded by its significance. He sat with his grandfather until he finally felt a buzzing on his wrist and found himself transported back to the present day, sitting in that very same kitchen with no one beside him.

He knew what he would do with the pocket watch. It would make a far better gift than the Time Traveler. It was not just his own history, after all. It was a significant piece of time, of place, and of memory. It should be passed down through generations, almost like time itself being handed down. He had learned that time was a kind of glue that connected the past to the present and that time travel was a kind of historical excavation. He also knew that time and time travel took place in circular rotations like a clock, rather than linear movements. Such thoughts about time travel, however, were better left for another day and another time. He had to find a nice box for the pocket watch before he gave it to his father.

# MAMA TRIED - BY MICHAEL A CLARK

THE MUSIC ECHOED DOWN THE PASSAGEWAY FROM THE COMMAND MODULE. PUJOLS TAPPED A CODE SEQUENCE INTO THE FUEL SUPPLY PLC WHILE squeezing exercise scissors between his legs. "The Grateful Dead did this better."

"Nah," I said. "Call me a fossil, but it's Merle Haggard's song."

I was monitoring the hydrogen/argon flow from the main tanks to the outrigger thrusters while working a wrist grip with one hand. We all exercised constantly, even while on duty. After what had happened to Dilip and how quickly he'd deteriorated, self-preservation drove us against the yawning effects of low-gravity space travel.

And exercise kept us from thinking too much.

The thrusters were Rolls-Royce, while the fuel storage tanks were Cryovac. A host of other manufacturers' systems transferred the fuel between, tracked the process, and delivered data to the ship's control center. That was the main selling point for the Mars Odyssey mission—big corporations would get government-backed contracts (with little cost oversight) to build the first manned space vehicle to leave Earth for another planet.

Of course, nothing had worked as planned.

"Is Kwai Chang holding up okay?" asked Pujols.

"I guess he's dealing with it…" I replied.

A tooth abscess on the first flight to Mars wasn't something Mission Control had planned for. Like all of us, Chang was checked over a hundred times for potential health conditions that might jeopardize the operation. We carried medical supplies, and we were supposed to be able to manufacture more as needed with the Stratasys 3DMach replicator system, installed with great fanfare. But antibiotics didn't pop out of the machine as easily as a screwdriver or a pair of earplugs. Chang's toothache had already consumed a third of our infection-fighting drugs, and we weren't even halfway through the Trip.

"Team, this is Todd." Our commander's voice muted out the old song. "Meeting in ten minutes, Rec Room A. Please be prompt."

"Todd's meetings suck," said Pujols as he recalculated the ship's fuel flow rate for the third time. "Smug, self-righteous prick…Ed, I don't like the look of these readings."

"Neither do I." I nodded.

I looked over my right shoulder at the viewport, staring at the vast empty outside. Stars were pinpricks where I could see them at all. And Mother Earth? I knew the exact distance from Her as we spiraled out toward the angry red planet.

"But this may be a chance to air some things out," I said. "And if our fearless leader calls off the mission and says, 'turn around'? It's only 46,783,421 miles back home."

Pujols looked at me, still working his legs. "Your sense of humor stinks."

The main rec area served as a conference room and a bunch of other functions, as it was the largest open space on the ship. The ceiling, laced with fiber-optic conduits, arched almost seven feet high. LED lights mimicked a 24-hour day/night schedule. The four curved HD screens on the walls would be the envy of a sports bar back home. Three of them ran ambient light patterns geared toward soothing overworked nerves.

The fourth screen was tuned to GoogleFoxNews, our main commercial link to human civilization. Tibetan separatists had exploded a driverless Uber bomb outside the FargoCitiSachs tower in Shanghai. A winter hurricane was flooding Norfolk, Virginia, again. The Salt Lake City Panthers would be playing Pittsburgh in the Super Bowl this Sunday.

I sighed. "The Steelers' defensive secondary sucks."

"Well, having Franco Harris's grandson as quarterback should help," said Pujols.

The heavier exercise equipment had been folded into cubbyholes in the rec room floor. Ipanema Lev and Malkin Yevgeni had put the three sections of the main table together, a pathetic potted geranium from the hydroponics lab at its center. Below our feet was the subtle turning of The Shaft, generating the modest artificial gravity in our long-distance runabout.

Guy Dewiley was coaxing a cup of coffee out of the finicky drink machine below one of the soft, cooing monitors. "Merde," he muttered as the semi-warm brown liquid oozed out of the dispenser nozzle with a sound like a chicken farting.

Geddy slumped in a chair, wearing a black MicroZon T-shirt. All our clothing bore corporate logos. Astro headbutted his leg, and the Canadian physicist hoisted the ship's cat into his lap. Our orange furball was scheduled to be the first earthling to land on Mars.

"I'm seeing things again," said Geddy, as Astro buzzed atop his crossed legs.

"Please. Do not mention this during the meeting," Guy said, wincing as he drank from his modified sippy cup. "It will sour Todd's mood. He needs to be upbeat while dispensing his motivational propaganda."

"God damn it, I'm not making this up!"

"No one said you were," Malkin said.

"Tunca checked me out. He said the test results were negative. I'm showing no neurological issues. But I *AM* seeing something!"

The three ambient video screens flowed peacefully. The news screen showed an anti-vaccination riot in Saint Louis being put down by armored police supported by drone gunships.

"Geddy, what is it that you think you are seeing?" asked Ipanema, our Israeli-Brazilian Ph.D. in psychology.

"When I turn a corner or walk into a compartment, there's something flitting right in the corner of my eye." Geddy stroked Astro methodically. "It's like a thin line, waving…almost in rhythm…"

"In rhythm to what?" asked Ipanema.

"I…don't know. When I try focusing on it, it's gone."

"Our eyesight's slowly deteriorating," said Malkin. "That's a known risk. I had to get a stronger contact lens prescription after only spending six months back on the Space Station." He worked a soft isometric sphere with both hands, like molding a snowball.

"No, Tunca checked my eyes out, and there was no sign of additional abnormalities," said Geddy. "Has anyone else seen anything…like that?"

"Wiggly lines dancing the rumba?" asked Pujols. "No, can't say I have."

"How are you sleeping?" asked Ipanema. A soft jet of scented air, smelling faintly of lilacs and green tea, subtly filled the room—another Mission Control-prescribed sensory method for calming stressed nerves.

"Not…well," Geddy replied. "Been having some weird dreams."

"I haven't been sleeping well either," I said.

Malkin, Guy, and Pujols all nodded.

"Hmm," said Ipanema. "Any odd dreams, Ed?"

"Yeah," I said.

"It's like episodes from a TV show," said Geddy, leaning forward while cradling Astro in his lap. "I can't remember what they're about. But it's like a sequence…"

"Hmm." Ipanema gently pulled on the tip of her nose.

"Sounds weird, but I kinda had that sense too," I said. "Snippets of people from times in my life. But who couldn't have been in the same place at that time with these other people." I squeezed my forearm, mentally noting the loss of muscle mass that almost nine months in space had wrought. "And it all seemed to be leading…somewhere." I sighed. "Its good hearing somebody else has been having them, too."

"Okay. I can see where this might be disturbing," Ipanema said, carefully rising from her chair. The ship's mild gravity meant we didn't float around like back on the Zero-G space station. But misjudging how much force you used to do something simple like getting up from a table could result in a painful accident.

"How about you, Ippy?" Malkin asked.

"I had some insomnia after we first launched, which is normal. But I can't recall any unusual dreams in a while." Ipanema drifted over to one of the HD screen remotes, velcroed below an isometric stretching station handhold. "Would you say these odd dreams are increasing the closer we get to…?"

She clicked the remote.

The news screen switched to a high-magnification view of Mars. It looked like a moldy Clementine orange, streaked with dark green lines and capped with a dirty snow cone.

"Nice timing," I said.

"I interned at i24news while I was at Tel Aviv University."

We stared at the Planet of War.

"That's what we came here for," sighed Geddy.

"Si," said Pujols.

We were Earth's best and brightest, picked for the greatest exploration in mankind's history, but after 249 days in this expensive tin can our bodies were eroding. Geddy was seeing dancing black spaghetti, and the rest of us were snapping at dreams. And poor Dilip, stuffed in a supply locker like a duffle bag of old clothes after his fatal accident. I wondered, not for the first time, why I volunteered for this goddamn trip to hell.

"And that's where we're going," said Ipanema. "Have anybody's dreams involved our destination?" She looked toward the screen featuring Mars.

I tried hard to think. Everybody else was trying, too.

"Nyet," said Malkin.

"I…don't think so," Geddy said, as Astro stretched a paw from his lap.

"No," Pujols said.

Guy gave a Gallic shrug.

"Ippy, am I going nuts?" Geddy asked.

"Are *we* going nuts?" I asked.

Ipanema smiled, slight dimples in smooth coffee skin. "*Nuts* is not medically accurate terminology. We are all trained professionals working in extremely stressful circumstances." She leaned against the ship's wall in a fashion model pose. "You've heard this before, and Todd's probably going to repeat it again in a few minutes."

"Da, but it's not working, Ippy," said Malkin, casting aside his exercise sphere. "We're starting to lose it out here."

"That's *definitely* not medically accurate terminology," she said.

"It's not just mental," Pujols said. "The fuel cells and the thruster controls—basic parameters are off, and it's not like the system's interface compatibility problems we've been having since launch. Ask Ed and Guy. If these readings are accurate, we could be close to crisis mode here. I can't quantify it in engineering terms, but the ship's whole technology seems to be…getting sick." He rubbed his forehead. "I don't know what the hell that's supposed to mean. Look, we're all supposed to be the Right Fucking Stuff, but goddamn it, I'm not feeling much like Superman right now. I'm starting to think we might not make it home." Pujols balanced his knuckles on the composite tabletop. "And I'm starting to not give a shit."

The ambient wall screens flitted between azure blues and verdant greens. One showed a large jellyfish, flaccidly flapping through a deep blue sea. I could hear Astro purring.

"We weren't supposed to go this far out," blurted Geddy. "We're too far away from Mother Earth."

"Geddy." Ipanema spoke carefully. "We all had our anxious moments in the run-up to departure. I did, too. And my reactions, *all* of our reactions, to the stress of voyaging deep into space were carefully monitored, analyzed, and effectively developed into a program designed by the best talent available so we not only *could* hold ourselves together and function for eighteen months in space, but *would* hold ourselves together and function and succeed."

"Did Todd draft that speech for you?" asked Guy.

"It's part of my job. One of the reasons why I'm here."

"You regret that now?" I asked.

"Like Pujols said." She nodded. "None of us are Superman."

"Da," said Malkin simply, as Mars loomed before us.

Todd bounced into the rec room, followed by Elise and Ryutaro. Astro meowed once and gracefully flowed from Geddy's lap to the floor.

"Hi, team! Thanks for getting together on short notice," announced Todd. "Tunca is with Chang in the infirmary, per safety regulations for a crew meeting." He touched a communications screen imbedded in the assembled conference table. "Tunca, Chang. Are you with us?"

"Yeah, Todd. We're here."

"How are you feeling, Chang?" asked our mission commander.

"Like I'm chewing sea urchins," replied the ship's taikonaut.

"We're all feeling your pain, Chang," said Todd. "Medical systems monitoring okay, Tunca?" The ambient screens around us now channeled conifer forests in bright sunlight, three-decade-old Radiohead playing subtly in the background.

Elise stood with tattooed arms crossed, her usual posture. Ryutaro, wearing a Tokyo Giants cap, was engrossed in the data interface beside the drink machine.

"I guess so," replied Tunca. "Todd, according to these medical readouts, Chang shouldn't have a headache, let alone a throbbing tooth abscess."

"I can *personally* tell you those med readouts aren't worth shit," said Chang.

Chang's real voice rang a split second after it came through the conference room speaker. The infirmary/second rec room was only seventy-five feet away down the backbone of the ship. Secrets were sparse here.

"I've got a high pain tolerance," Chang said. "Don't waste any more of the antibio stock on me."

"Thank you for that team spirit, Chang," said Todd.

"Todd, I've done a diagnostic check over the med systems, and I'd like Malkin or Guy to run it again, but..."

"Yes, Tunca?"

"I'm not real confident of the data. Like I said, the med diagnostics aren't picking up Chang's abscess. And another thing—according to the crew's personal monitor readings, we're *all* starting to suffer symptoms of hypertension, cellular vascular breakdown, and respiratory failure." Tunca paused. "Look, I'm not feeling this myself, physically. I think I'm feeling fine. But are the system sensors freaking out, or am I reading them wrong?"

"Okay," Todd said. "Malkin, can you help Tunca out on this?"

"Da."

"I wanted us to get together," continued Todd. "And I'll lead off by saying we all need to stay focused." He was clad in a dark blue full-body NikeArmor jumpsuit with the Pay/Book logo on his breast. Todd's Special Forces days were fifteen years past, but he was still the fittest of our crew of exercise fanatics. "We will be entering Mars orbit in less than two weeks. This is the critical part of our mission. We've all trained to be the best at what we do—"

"Everything is getting fucked up," muttered Geddy.

"Can you be a little more positive, Geddy?" Todd frowned on profanity.

"We were just discussing our joint mental and emotional states," said Ipanema. "Several of us have reported having odd dreams. There seems to be a general concern about how we're interpreting systems readout data, like Tunca just mentioned."

"Reported odd dreams..." Todd's pale forehead wrinkled. "Is there a technical or human factors issue causing the crew to have difficulty interfacing with the ship's systems?"

"That's debatable," I said. "Pujols and I were just working on the thruster/fuel cell heat exchanger flows—"

"Sometimes I stare at the screen, and the numbers *look* like what they should," said Pujols. "But...I'm starting to not trust the damn computers."

"Ryutaro, didn't you mention something about that a bit ago?"

"Yeah." Ryutaro's father had run a Honda Aerospace plant in North Carolina, and he had the accent of a NASCAR pit crew boss. Guy had dubbed Ryutaro "Bubba Sumo" early on, and the name stuck. "I've been reviewing the fuel/thrust transposition rates over the past six hours. Something's not right. But I can't tell you if the readings are inaccurate or if I'm just…not analyzing them correctly."

"What's *that* mean?" asked Todd.

"I don't know."

"I don't know *what*?"

Our commander had married into a conservative family made wealthy via door-to-door sales of cheap consumer goods by independent contractors. "Computers generally don't lie, Ryutaro," he said. "What are you saying?"

"I am saying that I don't know."

Astro leaped up onto the conference table, gently nosing around the comm screen over which Todd was hunched.

Elise glared at him. She hated animals.

"Okay," said Todd, pushing Astro away from the screen. "Tunca says that our individual monitors are reporting signs of biophysical stress. Please report how you all feel right now."

"Like hell," said Geddy. "And I'm seeing weird shit."

"Okay—"

"I've got a persistent migraine," Malkin said. "I'm having problems remembering things. I look in the mirror sometimes and…" He trailed off.

"I have lost my will to live, Todd," said Guy. "Only a bottle of 2021 Bordeaux and a dish of steaming fresh escargot can revitalize me."

"Very funny, Guy," said Todd. "Your sense of humor is still intact."

"That is all that's kept me sane on this passage without wine or palatable cuisine."

I had to laugh. The food plopped out by the 3-D replicators tasted like aspirin and cardboard. And alcohol? Forget it. Jeez, no wonder we were on edge.

"If we begin our approach at less than peak status, bad things can happen, fast," said Todd. "A lot is riding on us and this mission. The comm links will be getting more active the closer we get to Mars orbit. The whole world will be listening to us again, just like when we launched. You all know how much time, effort, and money has been spent to reach Mars." Todd's face was a mask of benign authority. "We need to show that the trust placed in us when we were selected for this mission was deserved."

"What's the 'official' reason that you gave for Dilip's death?" Pujols asked as he stroked Astro's ear.

"We all know what happened to our friend Dilip," Todd said. "I've prayed over his loss. The accident was something—"

"—that didn't have to happen. He didn't have to go out there," Geddy said. "That solar panel didn't need to be manually adjusted. We could have gotten by without—"

"Dilip, Ryutaro, and I conferred on the panel's condition, and Dilip volunteered to perform the space walk to repair it," said Todd. "We all know that was his area of expertise."

"I asked what the 'official' reason was that *you* gave Mission Control for Dilip's death." Pujols gently rubbed Astro's chin, eliciting a burble.

"I reported that Mars Odyssey crewmember Dr. Dilip Mather was impacted by a micro meteor while performing his extra-ship repair operation, sustaining injuries that led to massive cardiovascular hemorrhaging. I reported that the crew made every effort to revive him, but, despite heroic efforts, Dilip was lost to us."

The ship's metal skeleton seemed to flex with a sigh, and I wished it was just my imagination.

"That's not exactly what happened," said Tunca from the infirmary.

"He was seeing the same things I'm seeing," Geddy said.

"What do you mean?" Ipanema asked.

"We shared rest stations, remember? Dilip turned the corner into our bunk area as I was starting my shift. He froze, and I saw the look on his face. He saw them. The lines, dancing…I know he saw them." Geddy looked down. "Right before he died."

"He saw *the lines dancing*?" Todd pulled himself up to his full five-and-a-half-foot height. "Will someone please bring me up to speed on what Geddy's talking about?"

Geddy slumped back in his chair, his golden eyes coins of distant sadness. There was the thin humming of the gravity shaft coiling beneath us, the ambient screens flowing like advertising on the sides of slow-moving trains.

"When you turn a corner or open a door, they're like…thin and black, maybe two or three feet tall. You blink, and they're gone. But while they're in your sight, they pulse to a pattern. I don't know what the pattern—"

"*They?*" Todd's fingers knurled together.

Astro scratched his ear with a hind leg.

"What about the cat?" Elise asked. "Have you noticed if it has acted strangely during the times you've seen these uninvited visitors?"

"*His* name is Astro," I said. Orphaned by a Haitian earthquake and raised by abusive Scandinavian missionaries, Elise had a rough life. She was brilliant in statistical analysis and perpetually reserved. We didn't get along.

"Why are you asking that?" Ipanema asked.

"I did studies of paranormal phenomena involving lower animals at Duke's Rhine Institute while in my postdoctoral program."

"You?" said Malkin. "You *hate* animals."

"A sacrifice I made for my career. I was interested in the relationship between probability statistics and unexplained extra-physical occurrences." Elise slowly walked around the table, trailing a finger on its sterile pastel surface. "There have been numerous substantiated instances of animals ranging from frogs to killer whales reacting to what are loosely called paranormal events. In some cases, the animal's reactions to unseen phenomena have led to humans avoiding injuries or death. In *other* cases, they have led to humans' injuries. Or death."

"Like farm animals going crazy when a UFO appears?" I said.

"Yes." She glanced at Astro, then me. "You're more informed on this topic than I would have figured, Ed."

"My mom was really into *The X-Files* when I was growing up. I'd seen every episode by the time I was ten."

"People. We are on a spacecraft approaching Mars orbit in the year 2035," said Todd. "We are having difficulties with systems instrumentation, and we've already suffered one casualty. We do *NOT* have time to waste talking about nightmares, psychic cats, and flying saucers!"

"Yes, we do," Ipanema replied. "Todd, you said it yourself. We're nearing the critical approach point. We have to deal with *anything* that can adversely affect our mission."

"Are you suggesting that Dilip's death, Geddy's seeing things, and some of our crew not being able to accurately interface with the ship's computers might be related events?"

"It is within the realm of mathematical probability, Todd," said Elise.

"I've seen them, too," said Ryutaro. Everyone looked at him.

"So have I," Tunca called from the infirmary.

"Perhaps we should discuss these 'sightings' in more detail," Guy proposed.

"Okay." Todd looked like he was about to have an aneurism. "Let's get this out there. First off, why haven't any of you reported this phenomenon before?" He glanced at Ryutaro. "And second, what potential danger could this pose to the mission?"

"Did you want your chief medical officer reporting he was seeing *them*, Todd?" Tunca said.

"Or your chief engineer?" Ryutaro asked.

"I keep hearing these references to *them*," said Todd. "What is *them* supposed to mean?"

"I think you're asking if these are signs of intelligent life, Todd," Malkin said.

Everyone got quiet.

Kraftwerk hummed from the background screens showing alpine landscapes. Our planetary target, rusty and malignant, still engulfed the main display.

"That's what *I* think," said Geddy. "Either they came out with us from Earth or came onboard as we approached." He pointed toward Mars. "Whatever. They're here."

Todd settled into a chair and worked his temples with his fingers. "All right. Elise. What are the odds that Geddy, Tunca, and Ryutaro have really been seeing—"

"It is more likely we're harboring some intelligence not our own than it is that the crew have been suffering some collective delusion."

"Can you give me statistics to back that up?"

"I would estimate the probability at 73 percent that we have *passengers* who are not listed on the mission's official roster." Elise folded her arms again, a wistful expression on her face.

"So I'm in command of a spaceship bound for Mars infested by ghosts?"

"It's not always about *you*, Todd," Pujols said.

"Maybe they just want to help," said Chang from the infirmary. "We sure as hell could use it!"

Astro stretched out on the tabletop, yawning.

"So, what are we going to do?" I asked.

"We attempt to communicate?" asked Ipanema.

"Of course," Guy said. "Unfortunately, I did not bring my Ouija board along for this voyage."

"Maybe Todd could talk about his personal relationship with Christ as an icebreaker, eh?" said Geddy.

Our commander glowered.

"Geddy, did you say they move in a pattern?" I asked. "Ryutaro, Tunca, you agree?"

"Yeah," all three replied.

"Thin lines stretching and shortening?"

"Yeah, that's right," Ryutaro said, moving his hands up and down. "They kind of go like a rubber band."

"Peaks and valleys," Tunca said. "Repeating a sequence."

"Yep," said Geddy.

"Almost like dots and dashes?" I asked.

Todd caught that. "Ed, are you saying that *they* are using Morse code?"

"Can anyone remember the pattern from the last time you saw them?" I asked. "I did a thesis in grad school comparing 1990s-era Internet service with early telegraph networks. I *should* remember how Morse code goes."

"Ah…" Geddy reached for a ScratchPad and stabbed at the screen with his finger for a minute. "Just a guess, but I think they may have gone like this." He turned the slim rectangle toward us.

"Up the resolution and transfer that," I told Geddy, and a sequence of crude dots and dashes replaced the

Angry Red Planet on the main viewer. "Let Tunca and Chang see it, too."

"That looks familiar," Ryutaro said.

"Do we have a translation program for this?" asked Pujols.

Todd started working over the comm terminal. "We've got software capable of performing a myriad of tasks," he said. "Deciphering ancient telegraph messages…"

"So Ryutaro, this rings a bell?" I asked.

"Yeah." He scrunched his face. "But the lines were darker. Sharper."

"What's it say, Ed?" called Chang. We could hear him grunting as he shifted in the aluminum cage that was our sole hospital bed.

"Gimme a minute." This would have been a hell of a lot easier if Geddy had just transcribed 'S-O-S'. "Five…go…twelve…?"

"They're telling us to go back home," Geddy said flatly.

"Hold on, let him finish," said Ipanema.

"It's numbers," I said. "Coordinates?"

"Geddy, you didn't answer when I asked if the cat has reacted to *them*," Elise said. Astro yawned again.

"Any luck with a program to help me out here?" I asked.

"Ipanema, can you lend me a hand?"

"Sure, Todd." She moved to the comm port beside him. "Try indexing through the general cryptology folder. Yeah, that one."

Ipanema glanced around. "Well, Elise asked a question. Has *anybody* who's seen these…guests noticed if Astro can see them, too?"

"We may be about to find out," Guy said.

Astro was hunkered on the table, staring at a perfectly random space about three feet past my nose. His orange and white tail flipped lazily to and fro. But his ears were alert, and Astro was watching…something.

"There!" shouted Geddy. "By the envirosystems relay!"

"Yeah!" Ryutaro said.

"Oh my god," stammered Todd.

I turned slowly, as if hoping a spider wasn't dangling over my shoulder.

Five obsidian-black strips hovered below the ceiling, their sharp edges shimmering as if adjusting to a new environment. The dark void within each thick, unblinking line absorbed me. The black strips danced, dashing and dotting.

"What the fuck…" said Malkin.

"Geddy, does your Pod pick them up?" Ipanema asked.

"Yeah, I'm getting them!"

"Okay," I said softly. "Slow down. Fifteen…six…twenty-three…"

The black strips' pattern repeated five times, tight and smooth. Then they inhaled into themselves and vanished. Like shooting stars, as if they'd never been there.

Everyone froze. The side view screens played the theme from *M*A*S*H* and showed desert sand dunes.

"It's coordinates…I'm pretty sure of it," I said as Geddy transferred his shot of the lines onto the main view screen.

"Did that really happen?" shouted Chang from the infirmary.

"Yep," Ryutaro said.

Todd and Ipanema huddled over the comm screen. "I don't believe this," Todd said, breathing heavily. "I don't believe this…"

"They were giving us coordinates. For what?" asked Pujols.

"Landing Point Cheshire," Ipanema said, tapping the screen. "The touchdown zone where the Red Ball Express lands Astro, then launches him back up to us after ninety minutes on the planet surface. Can somebody confirm this?"

Todd was shaking his head, still muttering.

"Excuse me, boss," Ryutaro said. "Let me check it out." Todd nodded numbly as our chief engineer leaned over the comm screen. "Yeah, Ippy. It's Cheshire, about 350 clicks from Alba Mons."

"Ryutaro, isn't that pretty close to where *Viking One* landed back in, ah, 1976?" asked Malkin.

"I think so."

"Is that why Astro's supposed to go there?" Geddy stroked our cat, seemingly none the worse for this encounter with the paranormal. "They want him where Earth first landed on Mars?"

"Why would *they* want that?" Tunca asked from the sick bay.

"The odds are high that our visitors' communiques relate to both the previous *Viking* landing and the plan to have our Astro visit that site," said Elise. "*Why* is a question that will probably take some time to answer."

Astro sneezed.

"Told you she'd warm up to you, buddy," Geddy said.

"Maybe we should take a deep breath and think about all the shit that's just happened," I said. "Before we agree to shuck our mission parameters…"

"Maybe we already *have* 'shucked' them," Elise said with a slight smile.

"Maybe this is what our mission was really all about," Malkin said, nodding.

Ipanema gently touched Todd's shoulder. "Hey, Captain? We're going to have to make a call on what we do next. You with us?"

"Uh, yeah. We need a course of action. It's just that this is so—"

"*All* the events on this fantastic voyage could not be fitted into the planned outline, Todd," Guy said. "This just became another part of our mission."

Elise nodded. "We'll assume Ed's translation of the coordinates provided by the phenomenon is correct?"

"I'll buy it," Tunca said. Malkin, Pujols, and Geddy nodded.

"Should we accept what the phenomenon seems to be asking of us?" Elise looked at Astro as he licked his paw.

"You're in command, Todd," said Ipanema. "What do we do?"

Todd breathed deeply and then looked around the room. "I think the crew should take a vote."

We did. And we surprised ourselves.

The Red Ball Express was designed to drop Astro gently onto the planet surface and then launch its upper stage (containing our cat) back to rendezvous with the ship. The Express had an aperture that could be opened to the Martian environment, exposing Astro to its cold, dusty air for a few moments. It was hoped that much could be learned from our feline's brief taste of Mars, which would help the next mission put human footprints on the planet.

We agreed that our shimmering visitors wanted Astro's visit to be of a more permanent nature.

Our vote was unanimous, and we didn't spend much time debating the science of feline/extraterrestrial relationships. We loved our cat and would miss him, but we felt that letting him go was the right thing to do.

And so, with nary a dry eye but a quiet sense of hope, we bid our furry fellow traveler farewell. Astro willingly went into his capsule and down to the alien world.

Chang's toothache abated. Our bad dreams stopped, and the ship's systems felt normal again. We all got along better on the long ride home, like a huge burden had been eased off our collective shoulders.

Astro's vital signs reported strong throughout our trip back to Earth. And we never discussed whether we believed *those* readings, or not.

# THE ARCADE - BY JANELLE BLASDEL

AMBER LEAVES THE THEATER THINKING THAT MIGHT BE HER NEW FAVORITE MOVIE OF ALL TIME. SHE WONDERS IF SHE'S SEEN IT BEFORE—IF THIS IS A TRUE first or a false first. *Doesn't matter*, she decides, knowing she'd have loved it all the same.

She shuffles through the throng of after-movie bodies, everyone a little drunk and wobbly from the darkness of the theater, the smell of popcorn lingering, and licks the last remnants of chewy candy stuck in her molars. In the lobby, it is a symphony of pre-show anticipation: the hiss of soda machines and shouts of teenagers, swinging doors banging open and closed as one audience exits and another gets ready to enter.

Magic, really.

She zips up her coat over her scarf, pulls on her hat and gloves, and is ready to brave the Minnesota winter. She weaves through the long line at the InstaArcade, everyone waiting to clear their minds so they can watch something for the first time again and again.

*Searched the whole way back and just like that you were gone, gone, gone.* The memory of an old lyric says hello as she shoulders open the door. Those come as a surprise these days, remnants of a favorite song not yet zapped away.

Outside, the sharp wind whips at her face, and she coughs to clear her lungs, a steam-puff of breath rising in front of her. Transporters zoom by on Lake Street, full of students from the U heading toward Hennepin, where there's more fun to be had, but she's leaving the fun behind, walking to her apartment about a mile away. It's late for her—after ten on a weeknight—and she wants to be worth something in the morning. Worth something at what, she's not quite sure. For now, it's tutoring through Whimzie, but she's up for accreditation in the spring, and her numbers aren't where they need to be.

Her fingers are numb in her gloves—she forgot to charge the heat cells last night. She clenches and unclenches her fists and walks farther east, past her apartment. She's tired, but one session won't hurt, she reasons.

At Lake and Lyndale, she pauses and stamps her feet, waiting for the transporter lanes heading south from downtown to pause. Traffic's still busy, and, for a moment, Amber imagines herself in one of those transporters, a successful Wafer investor or maybe an engineer working on Gel. She'd be on her way home to a mansion on Lake Harriet, tired from the day, her auburn hair done up loosely in a clip. Exhausted but beautiful, she imagines her husband would say, telling her she needs to stop working so hard. And then she would respond, "But I can't. This project—it'll change the world if we get it right." He'd reach out and touch her face, pour her another glass of white—*no, red*—red wine, a pinot noir they would have had droned in that very night from Sonoma. She'd take a long drink and let her shoulders relax and—

"PROCEED! PROCEED! PROCEED!"

The cross-bot hovers next to Amber, ready to glide her across the street. Amber jumps, startled, and apologizes as she steps onto the platform. She holds onto the rail as it glides forward, heat rising from the vents below, warming her shins, working its way up her coat.

She walks two more blocks south to her favorite late-night coffee shop, Beans. The lights inside shine warm and welcoming, the front windows steamed over and frosted at the corners.

Bells jingle as the door closes. Behind the counter, Goldie with her glittering gold hair looks up. "Hey, hon," she says, and smiles. "Can I get you something, or—"

She sees that Amber is already shaking her head no and pointing toward the back.

"I'll ring you up after," she says. "Thirty?"

"That's perfect, Goldie, thanks."

Amber pushes through the swinging double doors and into a dim hallway with more doors along the right side. Above the first two, a red light. *Occupied.* Above the third, green. *Vacant.*

Everything in the room is gray. The walls, the table, the floor. Everything except the Arcade, a white box with a black screen. It catches Amber's reflection, her face thinner than she remembers, her eyes too big. *I look sad,* she thinks. She tries to cheer herself with a smile, but her heart's not in it.

In a flurry of static, she takes off her coat, scarf, hat, and gloves, and piles them at the far end of the table. She sterilizes her hands under the UV light and pulls an aluminum Wafer from the plastic wall dispenser. She unwraps it, tosses the cellophane, and places it on her tongue. She can't help but feel guilty, as though she's cheating on life, every time she uses the Arcade.

The screen lights up, glowing white. Her thirty minutes have started. Amber sits down, pulls her chair closer to the screen. She presses her palms to the silver handprints outlined on the Arcade. The palm-tops, or PTs, illuminate, and the machine flickers, making a connection with her that she must not break—not unless she wants her session to end prematurely. The hair on her neck, arms, even her eyebrows, buzzes with anticipation, the flow of electricity and promise.

An assortment of folders whir onto the screen, lining up into rows and stacks according to how Amber's brain has filed them over the years. Whether that's by location (beach, neighborhood, park), people (Mom, Dad, Lexi), or event (birthdays, holidays, vacations), Amber knows exactly where everything is.

Each person organizes their memories differently— there have been numerous studies on it. She's always wondered why her brain chose boring old files when her best friend, Lexi, uses galaxies with solar systems and planets, which, Amber thinks, is *very* Lexi.

Tapping her right finger against the PTs, she selects the folder labeled *Today*. She zips through, watching herself wave away her first WakeUp alert, then her second, then her third. She fast forwards to breakfast, an expired chocolate-and-peanut-butter-flavored goo pack that she eats while staring out her back window, overlooking a small patch of yard she shares with the rest of her building.

Next is a tutoring session with Shogo in Tokyo, which seemed to go okay. But then again, Shogo is her star student.

She moves her chin sharply left, fast forwarding quicker through the afternoon—a nap, a half-hearted yoga session in her living room, a glass of wine, another, and then, yes, here it is. Finally, the movie.

She keeps her palms pressed firmly against the PTs, the Wafer in her mouth getting hotter and hotter, as if it were a heat cube, those things people put in their coffees and hot chocolates to keep them warm.

This is the part of the Arcade that Amber hates most, the hot metal disc, but also the guilt of deciding which memories to keep and which to wipe.

"Don't they all teach us lessons?" she'd asked her therapist in their last session. "Aren't they all part of who I am?"

Dr. Gill had nodded, her sharply cut jet-black hair swaying back and forth along her chin. "Yes, I hear what you're saying, but what we've found is that people often feel empty because they crave new experiences. They have what we call *reality fatigue*— it's the same cup of coffee every morning, same bagel, same commute, same office chitchat, same dinner, same bedtime routine, same, same, same." Dr. Gill had marked each of these with her hand, one above the next, an endless ladder. "The world should be a place full of wonder and surprise," she continued. "Why not take the experiences you love and enjoy them with fresh eyes every single time?"

Amber supposes Dr. Gill is right. If you have the ability to get a thrill out of the exact same things every day, shouldn't you?

The Arcade hums louder, the electric current racing through Amber's body, rapid-firing into her brain, finding the pathway for *today, theater, movie.*

The movie comes into focus, as if she's viewing it again from her seat, but everything is sped up, every scene, every detail. She taps twice on the PTs with her pointer finger. The memory pauses, highlighted in her folder. She grabs a memo-screen from her purse and writes "Movie" on it.

She places her palms back on the PTs, resumes her session, and lifts her chin slightly. The movie memory is pulled into the foreground. With a sharp flick of her chin, she tosses the memory to the side, into the trash. A pop-up prompt asks if she's sure she wants to delete her memory. *Yes,* Amber thinks.

The PTs hum louder, a buzzing that sounds like a swarm of bees, suctioning her palms into place. There's a *zizz-uz, zizz-uz* sound and an icy-hot feeling that runs from the tips of her fingers to her wrists, into her arms and shoulders, up and down her spine, and then, in a few seconds, it's over.

The humming stops. Amber blinks hard and touches her temple. A slight headache blossoms behind her right eye. She wonders what she's wiped, whether she's made a mistake, made a decision too fast.

She grabs the memo-screen beside her. "Movie," she says, relieved. The Arcade screen continues to glow. Goldie hasn't closed out her session yet, so Amber decides to visit a memory.

She moves her chin quickly right to left, right to left again, scrolling through files from her past—summer camps, family weddings, her first studio apartment. But she knows where she wants to go already, has tried not to think about it all day, just like she's tried not to think about it every day for the past five months.

*Jonathan,* she thinks, and the Arcade reacts in an instant, serving up a new row of files. She thinks of their four years together and how the second year had been the sweetest, when they'd moved into an apartment together. Their love was still young, still exciting, but laced now with the promise of a future, of more.

From that year, Amber selects a random Friday night in October, calls it forward with a nod of her head, taps her finger, and sees Jonathan, his back to her, in their kitchen. She's sitting at the table working on a crossword. He's dicing tomatoes, ready to put them in a pan sizzling with olive oil and garlic, and Amber can almost smell it, *home.*

In these memories, he is so real and warm—his dark hair, brown eyes, and a little bit of scruff. She was teaching full-time then at a high school in the Kingfield neighborhood, southwest of downtown, and he was a product engineer at a med-tech start-up, both of them exhausted almost all the time, but loving what they were building together.

He turns and says something to her about the weekend, about going to a nature park where they liked to hike. Amber hears her past-self answer, and she wants to touch him, kiss him—wants to brush his hair from his eyes and smell him, that scent of pillow and sleep that was always at his temple when he woke.

Her palms are pressed so hard against the PTs that the muscles in her forearms ache. She holds her breath, not wanting to break this perfect moment, fragile as an ornament, but then the Arcade buzz quiets to a soft hum. The kitchen, their apartment, Jonathan's face all fade away, and the Arcade shuts down, the screen black again.

Amber blinks tears out of her eyes and rubs at her wrists, rotates them in slow circles. She tucks the memo-screen back in her purse, pulls on her scarf and hat, zips up her coat. She spits out the Wafer in the trash and gives herself five more seconds—only five— to think about that night, how good those nights had once been. Then she goes to pay Goldie, who will be waiting up front.

o

"I'M HERE TO SEE LIZ OLSON." AMBER STARES INTO the iris scanner and waits. A moment later, the glass doors slide open.

In the lobby, the Elders Home is pristine, with freshly cut tulips on every table and lightwells above bringing in natural light. Wrapped still in her winter gear, Amber quickly overheats as she walks to the tube—an egg-shaped pod with room for four—takes a seat, and says "Liz Olson."

The tube doors shut, and her mom's face appears on the screen.

"Hey, stranger!" she says. She's on her skywalk, bundled in a bright red coat, her hands bare as she scatters birdseed across the white snow.

"Hey, Mom!" Amber says. "I'm a little early. Hope that's okay."

"You betcha. I'll buzz you up."

And with that, the tube tilts back slightly and begins its silent, winding ascent to the ninety-first floor.

Her mom is at the door, ready to greet her, the color high in her cheeks from being outside and her short, silver hair as striking as ever. "I'll put on water if you want some tea, and here," she says, holding out her arms, "give me all that."

Amber untangles herself from her coat and scarf and hands everything over to her mom, who never seems to stop moving. Almost every memory that Amber has of her mom, she is in motion—sewing a Halloween costume, installing a backsplash, refurbishing a table—always a project to tend to while still staging properties and helping people find their dream homes and condos. Never missing a beat.

"Isn't it beautiful outside?" her mom asks, nodding toward the skywalk. She hangs Amber's things in the side closet, then bustles toward the kitchen.

Amber, smoothing her staticky hair back into a low ponytail, agrees and plops down on the sofa. She grabs a magazine and starts leafing through it. Trying to sound as nonchalant as possible, she asks, "So, how have you been feeling?"

Her mom, in a pristine white apron now, puts a tray of cookie pellets in the oven. "Good," she says, cheerful and light. "No big changes. And the doctor says my cholesterol and blood pressure deserve *two* rounds of applause!"

"That's great. And, um, everything else is okay? You're remembering things and...?" Amber's voice trails off, and she continues flipping through the magazine.

Her mom walks back to the living room and sits down across from her. "I know what you're asking, and I'm going to be honest, okay? My episodes are..." She hesitates, as if deciding something. "They're becoming more frequent, where I lose my train of thought or forget the name of something, like the fridge or telebot or whatever..." She looks over Amber's shoulder, out toward the skywalk, where birds continue to search for seeds. "It's scary, and it makes me sad about, well, everything, but I've started keeping a journal, and that's helped."

She pauses, runs the gold oval on her necklace across its chain, back and forth, like she always does when she's thinking. The kettle howls, and she springs up to get it. "But so far," she continues, talking over her shoulder, "those moments have been short-lived, and I always find my way back." She opens and closes cupboards and arranges china on a tray, the familiar clatter a comfort to Amber.

"Enough about that," her mom says. "How's tutoring?" She carries the tray to the living room, pours the tea, and drops a heat cube in each cup. The cubes spin instantly, the scent of orange rind and sweet spices filling the air.

Amber lifts her cup. "Pretty good," she says, nodding, feeling anything but. Yesterday, no matter what she tried, she couldn't stop crying, completely overwhelmed by loneliness and grief and then more loneliness. For dinner, she'd sliced an apple, then sat on the floor of her dingy apartment and eaten it, sobbing. But she can't bring herself to admit any of this to her mom, especially now, when it seems so important to make her mom believe she's doing just fine and will continue doing just fine indefinitely.

"How are the solar coils?" her mom asks. She takes a sip of tea. "Your place warm enough?"

Amber clears her throat. "Yeah, really warm. Sometimes I even have to open a window to let the heat out."

"That's a good problem to have."

"Mm-hmm."

Her mom tilts her head to the side. Her face softens. She looks at Amber carefully, and Amber sees the recognition there—of things left unsaid, but also the understanding of the need for space and time—a trait Amber has always appreciated about her mom. Her mom runs the oval back and forth across her necklace chain again. "Have you made arrangements?" she asks.

Amber tenses. She struggles to swallow what's left of her tea. "For…?"

"Well, for when you're an Upsettable for me."

It scares Amber how easily her mom says this, tossing the term about so casually. She feels nauseous, dizzy, but does her best to sound calm. "Oh, that. Yeah, not yet."

Her mom leans toward her and holds her gaze, hopeful. "But you'll do it?"

"I mean, I'm thinking about it."

Her mom reaches out, puts her hand on top of Amber's. "Okay, good, because there's nothing you should feel guilty about. You know that, right, sweetpea? I *want* you to do this. The thought of you going through everything alone, how painful that would be. I don't want that for you. Please."

Amber nods, the phrase *going through everything alone* a steady drumbeat in her head, *going through everything alone,* and she can feel the tears starting to form, the tightness in her throat, so she stands quickly and crosses the living room and looks out across the skywalk. "Those birds," she says, trying to focus on their lightness, their quick-moving huddle. "Must've been hungry, huh?"

o

"IT'S A VERY COMMON THING TO DO," DR. GILL SAYS. "Especially for the children of Alzheimer's patients." She removes her glasses, puts the temple piece between her lips, her now-it's-your-turn face.

Dr. Gill's office is modern and cold, with furniture that Amber thinks looks like the skeletons of what furniture should be. She shifts on the leather sofa, and it creaks beneath her.

Seeing that Amber isn't going to say anything, Dr. Gill replaces her glasses and presses on, gently. "I know it seems cruel or perhaps selfish, deciding to delete the memory of such a significant person in your life, but in my experience with patients going through this process, it truly is in the best interest of both parties, you and your mom."

Amber nods to show she's following along.

"You know, I used to be skeptical about prescribing the Arcade to delete significant memories—loved ones, traumatic events, entire years of a person's life. I worried about the long-term repercussions, but we've been doing this for a while now, and no other treatment comes close. You said that you use the Arcade recreationally?"

Amber nods again.

"What feels different to you about that?"

She twists a tissue in her hand, watching the bits come apart on her jeans. "Those things don't feel important, you know? They're just movies, or a really good dinner, or a massage or something. They're not my mom."

"The big things are hard."

*No shit,* Amber wants to say, but she knows Dr. Gill is trying to help her make some sort of progress. She sighs. "Yes, the big things are hard."

"What we've seen with these big things, though? When people delete them? Their happiness increases by forty-three percent, *at minimum.* After you do this, you *will* feel better."

Amber's arms and legs are crossed. She looks away, out the window to the slate gray sky, and lets herself imagine—just for a moment—what that kind of lightness might feel like, to no longer wake up every morning to the worry and dread and grief of losing her mom before she's even been lost. To let that all just fall away, how much easier everything would be.

"And your mom, she wants you to do this?"

She turns to look back at Dr. Gill, having almost forgotten she was there, and uncrosses her arms. "Yeah, she's been asking me for over a year. Says she's going to put me on her list of Upsettables as soon as she starts to forget me, so that, you know, I won't have to see her like that."

"And how do you feel about that?"

Amber laughs. "Well, not good," she says, and hopes that will be the end of it. But she knows it won't.

"No," Dr. Gill presses, "how do you *feel* about it? About being an Upsettable for your mom one day?"

Something inside Amber stirs. It starts in her stomach, a sick and hollow feeling that moves up to her chest. She tries to say something, tries to put into words how empty it all makes her feel—how bleak and bone-cold it is, as if all the light and warmth in her world has gone out—to know that eventually the person she loves most will *choose* to no longer see her. But before she can get any of those words out, that thing inside her breaks.

She pulls her feet up onto the sofa and sobs into her knees. "I don't want to forget my mom," she cries, her chest heaving and her breath hitching. "And I don't want her to forget me." She feels like a child, saying this while tears stream down her cheeks, but it's the truth—she's not ready to live in a world where she doesn't exist to her mom and her mom doesn't exist to her, and the pain of that thought is so sharp that she can't catch her breath.

Dr. Gill moves to sit on the sofa beside her, rubs her back, and tells her it's okay to feel what she's feeling. She takes Amber's hand and says she's going to give her the prescription if she's ready. "Do you want the prescription, just in case?"

Amber takes a deep, shuddering breath, her face a splotchy red mess. She wipes her arm across her eyes and nose and nods, and Dr. Gill pricks her finger

with a biodegradable microchip. It's there for her if
she needs it.

o

AMBER RUNS ERRANDS AROUND UPTOWN, HOPPING
on and off the glider at the post office, the library, the
dry cleaner's. The summer sun feels good on her bare
shoulders, and the sidewalks and patios are alive with
the energy of hardy Minnesotans who have survived
another winter and are gathering warmth for the next.
Maybe she'll go for a run around the lakes today,
try out the new cooling hood that Lexi gave her for
her birthday. *It'll definitely be hot enough for it,* she
thinks, sweat starting to bead on her upper lip.

She grabs groceries at Lunds, her last stop, and is
just out the door, getting her footing on the rubber
walkway to zip her up to Hennepin, when she sees
him walking across the parking lot—*him*-him. She
shifts the groceries in her arms and turns to walk
in the opposite direction on the glider, as if on a
treadmill, keeping her eyes locked on him.

It feels like such a long time ago now, a different
life, but she remembers the night that things went
bad so vividly—the sleeplessness of it, the gnawing
in her stomach. Whenever she'd been close to texting
or portaling him to ask him to come over, to come
back, she thought of the night she found out.

He'd cheated on her. Slept with one of his coworkers while they were traveling on business. Amber could still see his eyes, wide and insistent, when she'd confronted him about it, how he kept saying over and over that he loved her more than anything and this was just a stupid mistake, and they shouldn't let it ruin everything. "We can Arcade this," he'd said, trying to rush her out the door, "forget it ever happened." But Amber had pulled away. "No," was all she'd said. No, she didn't want to erase this. No, she didn't want to be with a man who could betray her like that. And he'd called her selfish. *Unreasonable.*

Now she sees this man in the Lunds parking lot, and the heartache and anger return. She sidesteps a woman on the glider and continues to walk against the flow. The groceries in her arms are heavy and awkward, and she's about to call out his name. *To do what? Confront him, yell at him, catch up?* When he turns toward her, his face is lit up, clear and bright. Her heart swells. That old love is still there somehow, and she feels stupid for it.

But he barely registers her. A glance and nothing more, and then he keeps walking, unfazed, toward the entrance. Amber feels so insignificant, so small, and it hits her—she's gone from his life, his mind, and he's free to live without the pain or sorrow or memories. She feels cheated all over again. For all the work and tears and grief she's put in, how much, really, does she have to show in return? Heartbroken once more, she stops walking against the glider and lets it carry her away.

o

"I'M HERE TO SEE LIZ OLSON." THE IRIS SCANNER flashes, but the glass doors stay closed. Amber tries again. "Liz Olson, please." The same flash, same nothing.

"Nurse's desk," Amber says, her voice strained.

"Hello," a woman's voice answers.

"Hi, hello, my name is Amber Olson, and I'm here to see my mom, Liz Olson."

Silence on the other end, and then the voice returns. "I'm sorry, but Mrs. Olson has moved all visitors to her list of Upsettables. I'm afraid I can't admit you to her room."

Amber's head buzzes. Her mouth tastes like Wafer residue. "Her— She did what? Are you sure you looked up Liz Olson?"

The voice is calm. The voice knows all. "Yes, Liz Olson. You're her daughter, Amber Olson, added to her Upsettables list last Friday night."

Last Friday night. That was the last time Amber had seen her mom. They'd had dinner, fish and chips that Amber had picked up from one of their favorite spots. It had taken a bit of time to remind her mom of who she was, but in the end everything had seemed fine—no worse than the weeks before. Why hadn't her mom at least told her? Surely she'd already decided, had made up her mind, so why not tell her? Then Amber would have known what to say, what questions to ask, how to say good-bye. She could have done it right.

"Please, can I just— Can I see her one more time?"

"I'm sorry, but no."

Amber takes a step backward and bumps into someone waiting to be admitted. *I'm dreaming,* she thinks. *This is a nightmare.* She turns away from the Elders Home and walks north up Nicollet to Eat Street. The smell of salt and grease is heavy and familiar, rooting her to this world even though she feels completely untethered.

*This can't be happening,* she thinks, and then Dr. Gill's voice comes to her: *Some life events are simply unfathomable.*

Bells jingle behind her as a door closes and the smell of coffee guides her toward the back.

*Some life events are so painful that they stunt our growth—they stifle our lives.*

She walks to the corridor of more doors where she's been told there is a solution, there *are ways to treat this.*

"Hey, stranger," Goldie says from behind the counter. "Thirty?"

Amber nods and keeps moving, through the double doors and to the Arcade, which stares back at her, the cold, blank screen. It all blurs together, the UV light, the Wafer dispenser, the crinkly cellophane. Her knees feel as if they might buckle, and she sits with a thud. She writes a quick note on her memo-screen, sets it aside.

She presses her palms to the PTs, and the Arcade whirs to life, her files cascading into a row. She thinks, *Mom,* and instantly, every memory that includes her mom begins stacking in order. Amber looks at them—all of them—as each animates briefly before another takes its place.

Her mom, spraying antiseptic on her knee.

Her mom, teaching her how to tie her shoelaces in the laundry room.

Her mom, singing silly songs in the kitchen.

The memories keep animating, and Amber hates them, hates what they mean to her now, the loss they represent, all this time together—learning and growing and counting on her mom to be everything to her. It *was* all too much to carry, a loss that no one should ever have to feel, and now no one ever did have to feel it again. *This is more than just the right thing to do,* Amber decides. *It's a gift she can do it at all.*

Tears run down Amber's cheeks, and she doesn't move to wipe them away. She flicks her chin quickly, afraid to pause too long on a single memory but wanting to make sure she glimpses them all—so many moments that add up to what seems an eternity, until, finally, she's at the end. Her last memory: last Friday night, her mom waving good-bye to her as Amber walks down the hallway, heading toward the tube.

The memory ends with her mom's face centered against the backdrop of her apartment. *You won't have to feel this anymore,* she thinks. *It'll all be gone.* She lifts her chin slightly and guides the folder of memories over to the trash. Her mom is still with her, but she's no longer with her mom. She hovers the folder there, her heart racing, tears streaming, and she releases.

*Provide prescription,* the screen prompts.

She takes a deep, shuddering breath and taps her finger hard against the PTs.

*Delete?*

She closes her eyes and pictures her mom one last time. She sees her standing on the back deck of their house drinking coffee, looking at the sky while Amber jumps on the trampoline below and catches her mom in this moment, unguarded and thoughtful. *This is a gift,* Amber reminds herself, and nods. *Yes.*

The machine whirs, and there's the same unpleasant feeling running up her arm, her spine, the hot stripping of memories, and then—silence, the screen blank.

Amber relaxes, removes her palms from the PTs. She's confused and rattled, doesn't quite know what she's done, but she feels better, lighter.

Beside the Arcade, she sees her memo-screen and grabs it. *Movie* is all it says.

She lets out a sigh. *Thank goodness*. She'd been starting to worry about herself lately, how depressed and lost she's been. She wipes her eyes and blows her nose in a tissue. She does one more check in the mirror and catches something in her face, a glimpse of someone she knows, someone familiar, who's been buried for a long time. Then she opens the door, ready for the long walk home.

# ABOUT THE AUTHORS

THOMAS BADLAN LIVES IN MANCHESTER IN THE UK. He has been an aspiring writer for as long as he can remember. He studied creative writing at Derby University and currently works as a teaching assistant in a high school. He runs a creative writing club after school for pupils interested in learning to write their own stories or simply improve their literacy and attends a weekly writers collective, the Monday Night Group, which has published an anthology of stories and poems. He has been published four times before, in anthologies from World Weaver Press, Future Fiction, and Eibonvale Press. He is passionate about speculative, historical, and general fiction and loves storytelling in all its forms.

JANELLE BLASDEL GREW UP IN COLUMBUS, INDIANA, and currently lives in Chicago, where she works in advertising and performs improv and sketch comedy throughout the city. She's a graduate of DePauw University and received her MFA from Southern Illinois University Carbondale. Her fiction and comedy writing have appeared in *McSweeney's*, *The Rappahannock Review*, *Main Street Rag*, *Slackjaw*, *Points in Case*, and *The Belladonna Comedy*. When she's not writing, advertising, or improvising, you can find her in a park hiking or a pool swimming laps very, very slowly.

GAVIN BOYTER IS A SCOTTISH WRITER AND FILMMAKER living in London. He has published two travel memoirs about running ludicrously long distances, *Downhill from Here* and *Running the Orient*. The latter book charts his 2,300 mile run from Paris to Istanbul, following the 1883 route of the Orient Express. Gavin's stories have been published in *Constellations*, *Blueing the Blade*, *DIAGRAM*, *Riptide*, *The Closed Eye Open*, *Bright Flash*, *La Piccioletta Barca* and *The Abstract Elephant*. He is also the writer-director of the 2015 independent film *Sparks and Embers*.

BY DAY, SUSAN M. BREALL HANDLES CASES INVOLVING abused, abandoned, and neglected children. By night, she writes short stories. Her stories have been published in numerous anthologies, including Running Wild Press volume 3 and volume 5, *The Raw Art Review*, Paragon Press's *Martian Chronicles*, *Impermanent Facts*, *Two Sisters Writing* anthology, *Dreamers Writing* volume 1, JewishFiction.net, *Feed Me Fiction*, and *Kairos Literary Magazine*.

SEAN CAMPBELL (WRITING AS S. D. CAMPBELL) WAS born in Canada's largest province, grew up in its smallest, and currently lives in its most western, residing in Calgary, Alberta. His first book, *Tin-Can Canucks: A Century of Canadian Destroyers*, was published in 2017 and covers the history of the destroyer in the Royal Canadian Navy. Sean's book *Before the Crash* is a collection of his previously published short fiction. Most recently, his short fiction appears in several anthologies released in 2021 and 2022. Sean currently lives with his teenaged daughter and the ghosts of several guinea pigs.

MICHAEL A. CLARK'S WORK HAS BEEN PUBLISHED IN *Galaxy's Edge, Liquid Imagination, Mystery Weekly Magazine*, Gypsum Sound Tales anthologies *Colp* and *Thuggish Itch, Tales from the Moonlit Path*, and *Cosmic Horror Magazine*, as well as the benefit anthology *Burning Love and Bleeding Hearts*. His short story "Scavenger Hunt" appears in the June

2021 Superior Shores Press anthology *Moonlight & Mayhem*. Clark grew up in Sharpsville, PA, a small town that's grown smaller with age. He now lives in Charlotte, NC, and works in industrial automation while spending as much time as he can outdoors. Baseball is his sport of choice, and he writes and records songs with workmanlike rhythms and lyrics. He likes both dogs and cats. Honestly.

**DYLAN CONNELL IS A WRITER AND PHILOSOPHER** whose work explores human psychology in relation to the troubled spiritual times of the modern era. Dylan has worked as a chess teacher, touring hip-hop artist, and private investigator. His stories have been published in *Penumbra, The Pointed Circle, ¡Pa'lante!* and other magazines.

**MARK EDWIN ELGERSMA IS AN ALUMNUS OF CENTRAL** Michigan University's English Language and Literature graduate program and has worked as an intern with the Isabella County Human Rights Committee. He is a writer of satire, science fiction, and literary fiction, and he has spoken at conferences about writing center work. In his free time, he volunteers with adult learning centers and humanitarian groups. He has been published with *Pedagogy, 101 Words, Toe*

*Good Poetry, Plain China Literary Magazine*, and *High Shelf Press*.

STEPHEN FLIGHT IS A NOVELIST, ESSAYIST, THEATRE director, and award-winning author of 30 plays (under the pseudonym Stephen Legawiec), including *Aquitania* and *Red Thread*, which won the Garland Award for Los Angeles Play of the Year. He lives in Maine.

WHEN HE'S NOT WRITING, MAKING MOVIES, OR penning songs, you can likely find Thomas Pace searching the alleys for treasures amongst the trash or doing a little urban bird watching. The band he fronts (The Thomas Pace Band) has been a staple of the Chicago music scene for decades, recording critically acclaimed music that often addresses politics and social justice. In recent years Pace has turned his energies to writing, producing and directing films including the award-winning shorts *The Lobbyists* and *Rain, Rain.* Originally from West Des Moines, and a graduate of the University of Iowa, he lives with his wife and their two teenage sons in Chicago's Edgewater neighborhood.

ANGUS STEWART IS HOST OF THE TRANSLATED CHINESE Fiction Podcast, a show which aims to save the world. His writing has seen occasional publication, most recently in *Waxing & Waning*'s 'Pandemic Panopticon' issue. He wrote "Meta-Shanghai" in Dundee, not far from the riverside, but by the time of its publication he will have fled time, place, and flesh.

JONATHAN WORLDE IS THE BYLINE OF PAUL Grussendorf, an attorney representing refugees, a former immigration judge and consultant to the UN Refugee Agency. His legal memoir is *My Trials: Inside America's Deportation Factories*. Jonathan Worlde's neo-noir mystery novel *Latex Monkey with Banana* was winner of the Hollywood Discovery Award with a prize of $1,000. Recent short fiction appears in *Antietam Review, The Raven Review*, the 2020 anthology *Ghost Stories of Shepherdstown*, in *Cirque Journal*, Ab Terra Flash Fiction on *Voices*, and *Stupefying Stories*. He is also a traditional country blues performer under the stage name Paul the Resonator, whose CD is *Soul of a Man*.

# ABOUT THE EDITORS

YEN OOI IS A WRITER-RESEARCHER WHOSE WORKS explore cultural storytelling and its effects on identity. She is obsessed with science fiction, where she excavates stories to expose and explore the permutation of culture across the genre. Yen is narrative designer on *Road to Guangdong*, a narrative driving game, and author of *Sun: Queens of Earth* (novel) and *A Suspicious Collection of Short Stories and Poetry* (collection). Her short stories and poetry can be found in various publications. When she's not writing, Yen is also a lecturer and mentor.

DAWN OSTLUND WRITES STORIES ABOUT technology's incursion on the rituals and traditions of different cultures around the world. She holds an MA in Politics, Media and Performance and an MA in Creative Writing. She lives in Los Angeles and works as an editor and proofreader.